Hunter: The Fallen One
A Lian Hunter Adventure

Lauren + Count,
Hope You Like It !
Larry Hagely

C. L. Hagely

Published by Rogue Phoenix Press
Copyright © 2016

ISBN: 978-1539765240

Credits
Cover Artist: Designs by Ms G
Editor: Sherry Derr-Wille

Dedication

For Madison, Dash, Zach, and Carrie, and to Morgana and Stephen, the light at the end of my tunnel.

Chapter One

The Descent

Descent-dɪˈsent Noun
1. the act of moving down to a lower place or position;
2. a road or path that slopes down;
3. the origin of your parents or other older members of your family;
4. the process of gradually changing to a worse condition;
5. a sudden and unpleasant visit or attack.

"Deep into that darkness peering, long I stood there,
wondering, fearing, doubting, dreaming dreams
no mortal ever dared to dream before."
— **Edgar Allan Poe**

Lian reached out in the darkness, his lungs burning from his heart racing. "Where am I?" He grasped at the nothingness in the air. His hand suddenly glanced off something sharp, and he could hear an echo of a voice beckoning him in the distance. He strained his ears to follow the sound.

"Lian, are you awake?"

Lian gasped as his eyelids shot open and the ceiling came into focus...6:29 A.M. As the time moved up one minute his bed began to shake, suddenly stopping as he sat up.

Lian peered out the window at the fog, which was so thick he could barely make out the ocean lapping at the edge of the beach. He looked down at his shirt and realized he was covered in sweat. Rubbing his eyes, he gazed across the room at a dark green jacket hanging over his desk chair. He studied the circular shape on the pocket-a large embroidered "A" with a small "T" formed inside. Outlining the "A" were three words written in Latin: *Academiae *Artes *Astronomicas.

He got out of bed and walked into his bathroom, turned on the faucet, letting the cold water run over his hands, and splashed water on his face. He quickly got dressed for school. As Lian was fixing his tie, he looked out the window and noticed the fog started to lift.

Parts of his dream were becoming clearer, the darkness...the sense of being lost. He grabbed his jacket, and headed downstairs. His mother Lailah was standing at the breakfast counter placing a plate of French crepes in front of the empty chair across from her.

"Morning, Mom," Lian yawned, stretching his arms over his head as he sat down.

"Good morning." his mother poured coffee into her cup and pressed her forehead to his without spilling a drop. Her blond hair was swept off her face with a small clip. Her skin was a pale milky white, and her delicate features gave her an angelic look in the morning light. Lian had always been told he bore a striking resemblance to her, although his dark hair, strong jaw line and broad shoulders were very much traits of his father.

"Has Dad already gone?"

Lian glanced up at his mom as he took a bite of a crepe. He picked up a taste of something sweet he couldn't quite place. His mom always liked to surprise him with a new flavor every time she made crepes.

"Lingonberry." She smiled after seeing the quizzical look on his face. "Yes, you just missed him. He had an important meeting this morning."

His father, Julian, always seemed to be working, either traveling to different countries or attending meetings when he was in town.

"Lingonberry? You got me on that one." Lian took another bite.

"It's Swedish." She continued to gaze at him as she sipped her coffee. "Is everything alright at school?"

"Oh, uh...yeah." Managing a smile, he added, "I was just hoping to see him before he left."

"Speaking of leaving, the car is ready for you," his mother said, as she picked up his plate while he was taking his last bite of breakfast.

"Alright Mom, have a good day."

Lian walked to the car, the backdoor opening as he approached. He sat in the backseat and looked forward at the console.

"Good morning, Lian Hunter."

"Good morning, Fila. We're picking up Gabriel this morning."

"Would that be Gabriel Stratus?"

"Yes, please."

"Gabriel Stratus, twelve point six minutes, ETA 7:34 A.M."

The car arrived at Gabriel's house on schedule, pulling around the circular drive to the door. Lian glanced up at the screen as Fila announced, "Gabriel Stratus residence." It was a large two-story white mansion with Grecian style pillars. Perched at the edge of a mountain, the expansive estate overlooked the ocean. As the door opened and Gabriel got in, Lian held up his hand to block the blinding sun reflecting off the house.

"Hey Lian." Gabriel smiled as he sat down.

"Hi Gabe. What's current?"

"Nothing much. Ready for today?"

"Yeah. Fila, Tri-Asterisk Academy, please."

"Tri-Asterisk Academy forty-four point one minutes, ETA 8:20 A.M."

"I didn't sleep too well last night." Lian still was not quite awake and figured it must be showing. Gabriel always looked so refreshed. His gentle blue eyes were soft, yet alert. His blond hair was perfect, not one strand out of place.

Lian looked out the window as they drove past more large estates, many in pastel colors of yellow or coral, and set back with wild flowers growing all around the properties. The road between the mountains winded around and curved as they slowly descended toward downtown Los Angeles. Suddenly the smell of salt water air was replaced by the smell of grass and shrub bushes scorched black from one of the many fires occurring every year. Lian studied the remains of some trees and what was left of a couple houses in the path of the fires. The car followed the curves, the headlights coming on as it passed through heavy dark smog making it seem as though they were heading into oblivion.

As they were stopping to get on the ramp, a homeless woman on the side of the road came into view. Lian saw her at the same spot a few times, but never paid much attention to her. A sudden knock at the side window made Lian jump. As he turned his head to investigate, a haggard face startled him once more. The woman was staring into the car, her head wrapped in a dirty cloth. Lian's eyes read her lips as she mouthed "Help me" through missing teeth, her outreached hand rose above window level. When they moved up another car length, he could see her torn and ragged clothes hung from her like southern moss. He also noticed her face quickly turned from a sorrowful expression to a nasty scowl as the car sped forward up the ramp with the rest of the traffic.

Right on cue, lady, Lian thought, recalling the face he'd seen from past mornings. Now he could see all the cars below heading up a ramp and stopping at a signal before joining the other commuters on their way to work.

He glanced up at the houses above the sides of the freeway. Most of them were old, small, and run down, and some barely seemed to be standing on their own. The buildings had aged to a dreary dark brown, and had thick bars covering their doors and windows, with the glass broken or missing out of many of them. The front yards stood out like colorful canvasses of trash-painted art, while more homeless people walked aimlessly around the landscape.

The car came to one more stop before taking another ramp, and Lian could now see a few large skyscrapers in the distance. They turned down a side street, and soon a large wrought iron gate was in front of them. The car stopped at a gray rectangular column, where Lian rolled down the window and faced the monitor. He continued to stare into it until his face appeared on the screen along with his name. The gate opened and the car moved forward.

Chapter Two

*Academiae...*Artes...*Astronomicas

Tri-Asterisk Academy's main building was a large three-story complex that spread across the grounds. A few other separate buildings were set further back on the property and spaced apart. A taller building sprung up behind the school shaped like a large mushroom dome. The academy felt like its own city enclosed in a fortress. The buildings looked ancient compared to all the other structures Lian saw in Los Angeles. Its dark grey washed stones had a scalloped texture that further added to the ancient feel of the academy. The stones ended abruptly at large pillars lining the entrance. A large engraved Tri-Asterisk symbol towered above the four doors.

Tri-Asterisk Academy was a private institution with a hefty tuition only the very wealthy could afford. Most of the Hunters on his father's side of the family had attended the academy, so it was expected he would carry on the tradition. He was happy when he heard Gabriel would be attending as well. It didn't take much convincing for Gabriel's family to enroll him since the school was known to be a doorway to the top elite colleges and universities.

Lian had heard stories about the school since he was a small child, but he visualized it so differently in his mind than what it actually was seeing it in person. Since this was his first year at the academy, he seemed to have more questions than answers. His thoughts moved back to the morning, and he wished he could have talked to his dad before he left for school today, even if it was just briefly.

Dark hedges lined both sides of the driveway, sharply trimmed in a continuous span of green. The car stopped behind a line of black cars, all with tinted windows so dark you could not see inside. As they waited for the cars ahead to drop off students, Lian stared at the three eight-foot-tall bronze statues standing in the center of the courtyard in front of the main entrance. All three statues faced outward and formed a circle, and the twelve-foot wings of each spanned out and touched the other two. As they passed by the statues Lian saw that each one stood on its own pyramid, and all three sculptures had human-like bodies, only with strange features. The one facing north bore the closest resemblance to a man, and in fact, would have passed for a normal human if it wasn't for its large outstretched wings. It had long hair and a beard, and was donning a fez-like crown, which gave off a god-like presence. Its hand was raised in some sort of gesture. The one to its right had an eagle's head, a feathered mane, and wings, all attached to a human body. Its left hand was holding a bucket, while the outstretched right hand grasped a cone. When Lian looked up at the face of the third statue, it appeared more menacing than the other two, with a dragon-like head, scales, much larger eyes, and a mouth curving up on the sides as if it was smiling. The fabric of the dome-shaped crown draped down the sides of its head to its shoulders where it touched a staff that was held there. It was obvious all three figures had some sort of symbolic meaning, but even more importantly, Lian felt a strange sensation that he had seen the images somewhere before.

The car stopped at the entrance, and Fila announced, "Tri-Asterisk Academy." Lian and Gabriel's seat belts unlocked, moved across them at the same time, and disappeared into the sides of the seats. The passenger doors propped open, they exited the car, and made their way up the large stone steps to the main entrance.

They walked together through the sliding doors and entered what looked more like a museum than a school. They looked down a wide entryway with expansive green marble floors. Achievement awards of the academy's excellence were framed and hung on the walls like artwork.

Ornately carved busts of past headmasters sat prominently on white marble podiums. At the end of the entry way stood a life-sized holographic statue. A large plaque beneath it read "Headmaster Avontis Gorvant." The headmaster's eyes seemed to follow anyone who walked by the statue with a simultaneous illusion in any direction at any time.

They turned down a corridor and into a long hallway flooded with green jackets. Lian looked up at a small black dome on the ceiling. *Eye in the sky,* he thought, as they joined the stream of matching uniforms.

All of the students seemed to wear their jackets proudly, a statement of the Tri-Asterisk elite and the privileged life they led. Lian looked down at his own jacket. To him it felt more like a constraint than a feeling of belonging to the academy. It was merely another means to conform and suppress individuality in his mind. He preferred his loose-fitting shirts and shorts like he wore at home and at the beach when he and Gabriel went four-wheeling. He looked back up at the haze of dark green making its way down the hallway.

Lian stopped in front of a large glass trophy case, and looked at a large gold cup engraved with the words "International Soccer League, 1st place." His eyes scanned over to the team picture and his father kneeling down on one knee in the first row.

Lian turned and caught up with Gabriel who was a few steps ahead, and kept pace with him as they both looked over at a group of girls who were locked in a circle by a doorway. One of the girls returned Lian's look, and as if on cue the rest of them turned and were now staring at him.

Girls, he thought. They always seemed to stay in their small circles, but here at the academy almost everyone stayed in their own clique. Lian turned and noticed Gabriel, along with everyone else, had stopped and were now staring up at the Tri-Asterisk logo slowly rotating above their heads.

Suddenly a man's voice announced, "As Headmaster, I would like to welcome students to another glorious day at Tri-Asterisk Academy. I would also remind you about our first soccer match of the season against Fair Gate Academy of Great Britain. I expect all of you will be attending to show support for our team."

Heavy classical music began to play the school's anthem as the logo continued to revolve above them. Lian had never seen the headmaster, who seemed to stay hidden within the school's walls. He looked down and saw everyone was pressing their two index fingers and both thumbs together in a pyramid shape over their heart as the music played. All movement in the hallway had ceased.

Lian looked over at Gabriel who shrugged his shoulders and made the symbol as well. When he turned his head and saw Professor Cordovak glaring at him, he quickly joined in. The music stopped after a couple of minutes and the logo disappeared. Lian looked around and noticed everyone had turned back to their groups and were walking to class as if nothing had happened.

"Geez, I can't believe they take the school song so seriously." Lian and Gabriel continued walking.

"Gotta love a little school spirit." Gabriel smiled and made the hand pyramid gesture again.

"Yeah, and nothing like a little pressure about our game coming up." They reached their lockers. "I just saw my dad's team trophy. 'First Place,' and not just first place, 'International First Place.' You know…the *big* cup." as he held his hands up in air and spread them far apart.

"Ah, don't sweat it, Lian." Gabriel patted Lian on the back, "It'll be great, just like it was in middle school."

"Well, that's easy for you to say. You don't have to live up to your dad's reputation." Lian held his face steady over the eye recognition scanner and his locker slid open. "You're lucky your father didn't go to school here." He put his bag inside and pulled out his tablet.

"True. But, if the truth be known, I'd rather disappoint my dad than Headmaster Gorvant." Gabriel imitated the headmaster's voice.

"Got me there." Lian laughed and shook his head as his locker slid closed. "Guess we better get to class before we're late."

They walked quickly to another corridor, and they both picked up speed when they saw the empty hallway. They stopped when they came to their Ancient History of the World class. A plaque next to the door read *Professor Irwin Snodgras.*

Chapter Three

Nine Wonders

Lian and Gabriel barely made it to their seats when Professor Snodgrass stepped through the door. A hush fell over the room as the instructor unloaded a binder and various books from his briefcase. At first glance, one might have classified Professor Snodgrass as homeless, minus the smell. He was a tall thin man, his long graying hair was a bit unkempt and hastily pulled back into a ponytail. His green wool suit jacket looked to be at least one size too large, and his tie was loose and fashioned in an uneven knot over his plaid shirt. He peered over his crooked glasses at the class, his steel gray eyes taking notes of missing students, mentally checking them off.

Many students thought Professor Snodgrass was strange and basically tried to avoid having any kind of conversation with him at all. Some would even call him derogatory things behind his back, including "freak", and "weirdo." Even so Lian and Gabriel knew he was a great teacher with very interesting stories, even if he did dress a bit strange, and brought up topics nothing short of eccentric. Professor Snodgrass often spun tales of his exploits as an anthropologist into his history lessons.

He had a passion for collecting oddities from his expeditions, and these strange artifacts completed the room's atmosphere. Jagged clear rocks, animal foot print molds, jars with preserved animals - all had their own special little nook in Snodgrass's domain, and some even lined a few of the bookshelves. Today Lian's eyes caught a new one he hadn't seen before - a reptile with a pinkish hue, closely resembling a human embryo except for the large tail that gave it away as something not human at all.

"Today we are going to begin looking at some historical monuments of the Nine Wonders of the Ancient World. Anyone care to name one of these monuments?" His long thin, almost bone-like finger pointed at the middle row. "Gabriel?"

"The Great Pyramid of Giza." Gabriel always seemed to know the answers to the questions Professor Snodgrass would pose to the class. He loved reading and studying history - the history of any era, any civilization.

"Yes, the Great Pyramid of Giza, consisting of over two million, three hundred thousand blocks weighing an average of two-and-a-half tons each. Just think of those astronomical numbers. Egyptians completed it by using Auditive Levitation. Tibetan monks moved large stones with this same method. Each of the pyramids also contained advanced technology."

Professor Snodgrass walked around the classroom, going through the other eight Ancient Wonders - the Hanging Gardens of Babylon, the Statue of Zeus at Olympia, the City of Atlantis, the Temple of Artemis at Ephesus, explaining why each had an important place in ancient history. He continued on with discussions about the Mausoleum at Halicarnassus, Gobi - the City of Gold, the Colossus of Rhodes, and the Lighthouse of Alexandria. His steadfast stare pierced the back of the room. He then turned abruptly on his heels and walked back to the front of the classroom. Some students were taking notes, others were yawning, and a couple more were snickering as the professor walked by.

Snodgrass arrived at the front of his desk, sat down and folded his arms, his stare now focused on the floor. He paused for several seconds before looking up at the students. "So, next time we meet, we will experience the brand new technology the academy has just purchased. In the meantime, please read the fourth chapter on Sumer, just so you can attain some background information on what you are going to see." Professor Snodgrass stood up, and slowly walked behind his desk. "Any questions?" He pushed his belongings back into his briefcase and binder.

Glancing up and seeing no response, he announced, "You may leave at the bell," and left as quickly as he came in.

As Lian turned around to gather his books, he locked eyes with Annaka Dimortra, and suddenly froze. He caught a flash in her eyes that flickered as she swept her long black hair off her shoulder, and then blinked - all of which seemed to be happening in slow-motion. Immediately, a chill ran up his arms. She seemed to have this unique way of looking directly at you, like she was reading you off a page of literature. Lian sensed this strange attraction toward her, a magnetic force whenever she was near. The bell rang, and immediately he felt something lift from him, as if Annaka's stare released him as trying to get his attention this whole time.

"Hey, are you okay?" Gabriel looked concerned.

"Yeah, yeah...let's go." Lian felt a bit flush, and turned just in time to catch Annaka walking out of the classroom. He noticed a strange grin on her face, a look like she'd won. But won what?

Chapter Four

H.A.R.T.

Lian walked down the long corridor, passing by a couple of seniors in the hallway. The upper-classmen, especially the seniors, always looked so menacing every time he saw them. First of all, their size was intimidating, because they towered over all the other students. Those differences of height and weight, and basically the overall size of students were uniform with every grade. Every lowly freshman was smaller than any student in an upper class.

Besides the size factor, the seniors also seemed to possess something very secretive, a mysterious aura noticeably different from any other students. Lian couldn't pinpoint why that feeling struck him as it did. There was nothing concrete about the strange sensation that kept nudging him, kept coming back, each time a little stronger.

As he entered his astronomy class, Lian turned his head just in time to see a senior make a gesture with his index and pinky finger raised up in the air to a passing classmate. *Seniors,* Lian thought as he made his way to his seat.

Professor Lovitt was a beautiful lady. A compilation of very striking features including crystal eyes and long blonde hair. In many ways she reminded Lian of his mother. She was so lady-like, but athletic…soft-looking, but intense. These contrasts made it hard for Lian to concentrate on anything she was teaching. As beautiful as she was, her looks couldn't compare to how genuinely nice, gentle, and understanding she was with each and every student.

She finished setting up her computer for the lesson, and began a very sultry walk between the desks, touching each one on her left, then her right as she made her way slowly down the row. When Professor Lovitt got to the end of the row, she gracefully turned around. Every set of eyes had followed her all the way to the back of the classroom.

"My very excellent mother just served us nice pies now." Professor Lovitt looked around the class-each student now donning a confused face about her statement. "Today we are going to discuss the planets that make up our solar system." She turned and moved slowly to the right side near the front of the room, and pointed to a large chart. "Our solar system," the professor picked up a laser pointer near the side of the chart, "starting with the inner-most planets closest to the Sun, we have Mercury, Venus, Earth, Mars, and Jupiter." Professor Lovitt's soft voice continued, "As we move on to the outer planets, we have Saturn, Uranus, Neptune, Pluto, and Nibiru."

"So, do you see now?" Lovitt put the laser on the planets one at a time as she went down the list, "My Very Excellent Mother Just Served Us Nice Pies Now. You can use that mnemonic device to memorize the order of the planets. I imagine it would help if you like pie."

The students laughed softly in unison.

"I hope this chart was useful for any of you who learn best in a two-dimensional framework. Now, I believe the same opportunity should be given to those who prefer an additional dimension and a little more heart, please excuse the pun. This "H.A.R.T." – which is spelled H-A-R-T, is an anagram for "Holographic Automated Reality Technology." Professor Lovitt reached down and pressed a small button on the belt around her dress, and a huge hologram of the universe appeared above the classroom. "Ahhhh...that's more like it. What do you think?"

A hush fell over the room. Lian's eyes fixated on the hologram swirling above them. The details were astounding-a hundred billion stars and galaxies seemed close enough to touch.

"Okay, we are now going to move at super light speed, so watch carefully."

The professor pushed another button and the holographic view raced through the universe, producing a feeling similar to the ups and downs and quick side movements, which reminded Lian of a hover coaster ride. It all came to a sudden stop, forcing Lian and the rest of the class to jolt forward involuntarily. He looked up as a planet came into sharp focus–every mountain, every crater.

"That was quite exciting, wasn't it? Normally, we won't be taking such quick trips to planets, but I thought the first time I'd make it special. Okay, I know it looks a little different so close up, but this is Pluto. For a short time, astronomers actually dismissed Pluto, changing its classification. It claimed it was just a dwarf planet, and part of the Kuiper Belt which contains at least a trillion comets. However, a more powerful telescope was able to define Pluto as a planet once again, and its satellite, Charon, helped with the planet's reclassification."

Professor Lovitt used a laser pointer again as she highlighted some of the details of the planet. This time Lian noticed the laser seemed to be coming out of her finger as she pointed.

"I want to make one more stop before we leave the galaxy here today."

The view moved out from Pluto, and the planets zoomed by once again, and then stopped at the fourth planet from the sun. "Most of you are familiar with our first colonized planet, Mars. Maybe some of you possibly have relatives living there? Anyone?" Professor Lovitt looked around as a few hands darted up in the air. "Mars had once supported life, and with a little help has regained that ability yet again." The planet spun slightly in front of them as Professor Lovitt raised her hand up. "Here is Utopia 23, one of our living centers full of bustling activity. I wouldn't mind retiring there myself one day."

Lian looked at the buildings of the large city surrounded by red mountains and crevices of water. It looked like any other city he'd seen, except for the way the buildings all connected together in a maze-like pattern. There was something also very sterile looking about the environment that reminded him of a science lab.

A massive mountain jetted into the skyline, casting a dark shadow over the encroaching city.

"That looming monstrosity is Olympus Mons, the largest volcano in our solar system." Professor Lovett's eyes shifted slowly around the classroom, "Seventeen miles high and spanning over three hundred-twenty miles wide." She pivoted on her heels as she turned her gaze back up at the hologram, "Now *that*...is a volcano. Luckily, it has been inactive for quite some time. Now I am going to pull back so you can see a glimpse of all the planets in the order we discussed." Once again all the planets came into view lined up horizontally, and Professor Lovitt talked in a very drawn out way, placing emphasis on each word. "Notice the different sizes of the planets...the colors, the rings...all of them unique in their own magnificent way."

Lian was mesmerized by the sight of all the planets that seemed to dangle before them in the infinite blackness. He recognized Saturn with its massive rings encircling the planet. Jupiter, Uranus, and Neptune also had rings, but they were minute in comparison. To the right of those he recognized Pluto again.

"If you look to the far right and at the last planet Nibiru, you will notice it appears to have wings instead of rings. That is an easy way to remember the planet Nibiru, "Wings, not rings." They are not wings obviously, but we will study what actually causes this illusion when we get to that planet. It is a complex one to study and understand, so we are going to wait until later to learn about it."

As Lovitt made her way back to the front of the classroom, the holograms slowly disappeared. "Our next class will be in the new observatory, where we will learn about Neptune, our third outermost planet, and some constellations."

Chapter Five

The Pleiadians

Lian and Gabriel walked into the cafeteria. It was a large open area with circular tables surrounding an obelisk-shaped fountain. Three figures made of pentelic marble stood in the center. They saw Jimmy eating by himself at a table, so they decided to drop off their backpack there before getting in line.

Jimmy went to middle school with Lian and Gabriel. He was a very thin boy with curly brown hair sticking out in every direction, and large front teeth he seemed to be very self-conscious about. He always covered his mouth when he laughed or smiled. Jimmy was also awkward, and Lian and Gabriel always tried to help him when they could. They saved him more than a few times from some of the grade school bullies.

"I could really use this class today. Lunch is the one class I'm really good at." Jimmy smirked as Lian and Gabriel grinned in unison. "You'd think they would serve better grub with such a hefty tuition," Jimmy grumbled, his mouth half full of food.

"I'm surprised anyone has an appetite in here." Lian looked up at the figures in the fountain. Each of the three haunting figures had hollow eyes and panged expressions. Water gushed from their agape mouths, and their arms were held out in a protective stance as if they were shielding themselves from some impending doom.

Gabriel noticed Lian's fixation on the marble figures, and pretended to talk into a microphone, speaking in a deeper and louder voice like an announcer, and pointed at the fountain. "And The Guardians will come to save the world...save mankind."

"The Guardians?" Lian looked over at Gabriel.

Jimmy looked at both of them with his eyes wide and made a gulping sound as he swallowed.

"Yep. This fountain depicts the apocalyptic eternal battle between the Pleiadians and the opposing forces in the world. Basically, it's a conflict between good and evil here on Earth actually starting on the planet Nibiru."

"Well, that's depressing." Lian and Gabriel continued looking at the fountain in silence.

"Speaking of depressing, did you guys hear about Kate Farris?" Jimmy took another drink.

Lian looked over at Gabriel who shook his head. "No, what happened?"

"No one seems to know." Jimmy brought his backpack up from the seat, and set it on the table. "I heard she's been missing for over a week."

Lian knew Kate from his math class. She was a short blond-haired girl who wore glasses with thick black frames. A bit shy, but appearing rather studious, she always sat in the back of the room during math.

"Maybe she just ran away." Gabriel stood up. "I'm sure they'll find her."

Lian nodded his head in agreement, but something in his gut told him something wasn't right. She didn't seem like the type of girl who would rebel or just run away.

"Hey, going back to the subject of "grub", I'm going to get some myself. Want anything Lian?"

"Nah," Lian shook his head. "I think I lost my appetite." Lian looked over at Jimmy who just remembered his project and pulled out his tablet from his backpack.

"It really has you worried, huh?" Lian watched Jimmy frantically writing notes on his tablet. He was surprised to see Jimmy would be attending Tri-Asterisk since he always seemed to fall behind in his work all through elementary and middle school. Professor Cordovak's class would not prove to be any different for him. It seemed Jimmy was falling more and more behind every week.

Jimmy let out a sigh. "I just can't keep up with Professor Cordovak. She won't approve any of my project ideas. She keeps saying I wasn't paying attention, but I was." He shook his head slowly, "Maybe this school is too much for me. It's not only the lab. It's all the classes here. They may as well be in a different language as much as I am getting out of them."

Gabriel sat back down with his tray and took a large bite of food.

Lian looked at Jimmy who seemed close to tears, and he wished he could be of more help. "Jimmy, I'd be more than happy to help you, to tutor you if you need me to. All you have to do is ask. You know that."

"That goes for me, too. Anytime you need help, we're there for you," Gabriel chimed in while scooping up another bite of food.

"I tell you…I don't think it's fair Professor Cordovak chooses who we work with in science."

Lian looked across the lunch room at his lab partner Calek, who was sitting stiffly at a table about ten feet from them. "At least you were assigned a nice looking girl to work with you, Jimmy. You're both lucky you aren't stuck with Frankenstein over there." Lian motioned toward Calek with his head.

"Frankenstein's monster." Gabriel took a bite of an apple. Lian and Jimmy both stared at him oddly.

Gabriel finished chewing while looking at one friend and then the other. "You mean Frankenstein's monster. Frankenstein was the name of the doctor." His two friends kept looking at him. "He made the monster out of reanimated body parts he got from various corpses," he added, taking another bite of apple. Lian and Jimmy looked at each other and then back at Gabriel. "Geez, don't you guys ever read? I thought everyone knew that."

"Yeah, we read. But we must have missed that important piece of information," Lian retorted as Gabriel let out a sigh and cocked his head sideways at Lian. "And besides…no one reads as much as you do, Gabe."

"Touché." Jimmy pointed at Gabriel, and they all laughed.

Chapter Six

The Silent Partner

Professor Cordovak was a menacing woman. Her hair was pulled back in a tight bun at the nape of her neck. She always seemed to wear black, and even had a black modacrylic lab coat she always wore during lab days. You could catch her looming over the class, even poking her head in between lab partners at each lab table to examine the students' progress.

"If anyone needs help with their labs, please do not hesitate to ask. Please do not put this off, and especially do not wait until the last minute to approach me for assistance," she instructed.

She stared down at Jimmy as she passed his desk, glaring at him for a few seconds, although her stare seemed to last a lot longer in Jimmy's mind. He responded by sliding a little further down in his seat, his face changing from a pale white to a deep shade of red.

Lian felt bad for his longtime friend. Jimmy was already having a hard time keeping up in a couple other classes, even though school just started a couple of weeks ago. In Professor Cordovak's class, he was falling further behind with every assignment. The first project of the year in science class was coming up on Friday, and that assignment just added to Jimmy's woes.

"Alright, I want everyone to move to your designated lab tables with your assigned partner. Make sure you have your lab manuals with you," commanded Professor Cordovak. "Today we are going to learn how to blend chemical compounds. You will be expected to catalog and remember in which order the ingredients are added, in addition to the specific effect each chemical makes as it is blended into the solution. Finally, you will need to write a detailed description of the final result in your lab manuals, namely what appearance this solution has, the colors involved, the odor emission, the movement within the beaker, if any, and the final measurement in milliliters. In that manual entry you will include a general hypothesis of what this compound could be used for in the scientific community. Remember, keep careful and precise notes during this experiment, and work as a team with your partner," Professor Cordovak sat down behind her large desk, "this will greatly increase your efficiency and productivity."

Lian looked around the room as he walked toward his assigned lab table. Professor Cordovak's science lab was a visual blizzard of white, a very cold flat white. The walls were white, the ceiling was white, even the lab tables were a shiny, metallic white. The matrix polyurethane floors were all white, except for a small black circle where the intersecting lines met at every square foot. The room was a sharp contrast to the professor's black hair and clothing, making Cordovak's outward appearance seem even a deeper darker black. The melamine resin lab tables were arranged in perfectly aligned rows, with each table holding two people and equipped with a Bunsen burner, sink, and a built-in test tube and beaker holder.

The lab tables were also designed so partners would sit on affixed stools across from each other, but off-set at opposite sides of the table. Lian figured this was to discourage copying. He looked over the different size tubes and beakers, graduated cylinders, mortars and pestles, and other chemistry paraphernalia lined in the center of his table. He opened his lab book to today's lesson with the different names of the compounds.

He glanced briefly at Jimmy who sat two rows over, and wished he could have drawn him as a partner, mostly to help him in case he ran into trouble with an assignment. Unfortunately, Professor Cordovak had a knack for deciphering early on which students were friends, and those students were never assigned as partners. Lian wound up with Calek, and

Jimmy was teamed with some girl. The only reason he knew his partner's name was because he heard Cordovak call it out during roll call every day. Not one word ever left Calek's mouth during science class so far this school year, even though Lian tried to be friendly with him on more than one occasion.

Lian was well aware Professor Cordovak's assignments would be much easier to do if the assigned lab partners would team up, especially since it was announced early on some of the experiments would contain very strange chemicals and dangerous elements. Knowing two sets of hands to perform the experiments properly would only be possible if Calek and he could find some common ground, Lian recalled an old proverb, "You can lead a horse to water, but you can't make it drink".

Professor Cordovak eyed the class with a hawk-like stare, sneering and making sounds of displeasure as she walked around looking at the class, examining each of the lab tables and the students' progress on the assignment. Lian glanced over at Calek as he grabbed a couple of jars and started mixing the compounds. His dark hair was cut short and parted stiffly to the side. He noticed Calek always sat so straight and rigid, in an almost military posture. He suddenly turned toward Lian, and after a quick exchange of eye contact, he looked down at the table directly in front of Lian as if to say, "Quit looking at me." Lian ignored Calek's body language and grabbed a mortar and pestle, a graduated cylinder, and a beaker, and started on the assignment.

"No help from you today suits me just fine," Lian muttered to himself. He knew this assignment was not going to be a hard one to do anyway.

"What do you think you are doing, Evans?" Professor Cordovak squawked. "You *do* have your manual in front of you, *don't* you? You *do* have an idea how to measure a milliliter, do you *not*?" As Evans started to stutter an explanation of how he spilled some chemicals, the professor put an end to it. "Miss Tyler, *you* are his lab partner. You are *supposed* to keep each other on track." Her eyes darted quickly around the room. "And that goes for everybody. Do you hear me?" Students who stopped working to witness the trouble Evans was in, immediately scampered back to their projects.

Near the middle of the period, his lab partner seemed to have already completed the assignment, and began cleaning up his area. Lian caught a glimpse of a Band-Aid near his hand, just barely peeking out of his shirt sleeve, and what looked like a pile of dandruff or some other flakes were scattered all over Calek's work area. As his partner continued to clean his beakers, Lian paid no attention to this development, and scanned down his lab book for the rest of the compound order.

When the solution starts to turn green, add 3.5 mL of the AL/PB mixture from step 11. Save the rest of the mixture for the final step. The solution will now appear silvery in nature. Shake the beaker slowly in small circular motions until the solution is fully mixed.

That seems simple enough, Lian thought. He read on.

Prepare and carefully add .78 mg of Cy-G, followed immediately by 2.4 mL of ZZ in liquid state. Do not shake. Remember to keep heat on the ZZ element during these other steps to alter its natural state at room temperature.

Lian finished preparing the compounds in the correct order, carefully jotting down notes as he progressed through the assignment. He poured them into his beaker, and took a step back to admire the glowing silver concoction with perfectly-spaced red stripes running through it. Glancing up, he saw Professor Cordovak also looking at his shiny solution from across the room. She put a check by Lian's name on her black polycarbonate clipboard, and then nodded at him, allowing one corner of her mouth to move slightly upward. Surmising this reaction would be about as close to a smile and as good as it gets with the professor, Lian smiled back as he finished recording his procedures and results in his lab manual, and started cleaning his area.

Out of the corner of his eye, Lian caught Calek pulling out his mortars and beakers once again. His beaker solution had turned to a swirling black. *What's this?* Lian thought. *Did my brilliant, stuck-up lab partner forget to do something? Well, he will be getting his ultimate just deserts if that is the case.*

Ignoring what Calek was up to on the other side of the table was just not good enough for Lian today. He had to see the end result of Calek's good idea-gone bad with this assignment. He couldn't tell what the exact problem was from the mess on Calek's table, but he did know his lab partner was out of time when the bell rang. Lian hung his last beaker in its proper spot, and walked over to put his lab manual on Cordovak's desk. He looked back and started grinning as he saw the professor walking over to Calek, who was frantically measuring, pouring, moving lab equipment around, and erasing things in his manual.

I wonder how he feels now about going solo the rest of the year, thought Lian, as he pushed open the double doors of the science lab and walked out.

Chapter Seven

The Match

As Lian and Gabriel put on their soccer uniforms, Lian's thoughts were somewhere else. All the other players were talking about their first game versus Fair Gate, an international team from Britain. Lian and Gabriel both played soccer since they were six years old. They both enjoyed the sport and it was always a source of escape for Lian when he played. Soccer created another world with the adrenaline rush of holding the ball so close to his feet, guarding it, passing it to a teammate, and the ultimate thrill of the game-scoring.

Today, Lian's mind kept replaying Calek's flaky skin, his bandages, and his more than weird and secretive behavior. He was tying the laces of his cleats while tying thoughts together to make sense of the whole story behind his lab partner. He knew Calek's brother Salem had been involved in some strange incidents at the academy, but Salem never seemed to act as weird or as unfriendly as Calek, at least as far as Lian could surmise from a distance.

His mind now shifted gears and he worried about playing well enough today to live up to his father's expectations. He started paging through other recent memories of strange happenings, and stopped at Annaka and the way she made him feel. Lian couldn't explain that either. He couldn't help but wonder if all the strange things he had been seeing and feeling lately were connected. Were some of these weird events actually from his imagination or coming alive from bits and pieces of his dreams? As hard as he tried, he couldn't connect the dots.

"It's going to be a great game." Gabriel smiled as he gave Lian a pat on the back, bringing him back to reality. "I wonder how good the other team is. I would imagine the British really make all of their players train hard at soccer...their game of football, at least from what I've heard about their schools." Gabriel shut his locker as he watched Lian allow his mind to wander off somewhere else again. He then stood up and started stretching his legs, and lightly punched Lian in the arm. "Lian. You've got to get ready for the match. You know, I really think you should let all these other things go for now and just concentrate on soccer. Come on, let's enjoy the game."

"Yeah, you're right." Lian quickly returned from his thoughts. He closed his locker and glanced up at Gabriel. "Let's see what this other team's got."

Lian stood up, grabbed one of the soccer balls and bounced it off his knee over to Gabriel, who quickly responded with a head butt of the ball. It shot back at Lian who caught it easily right in front of his face. He moved his head around the ball and grinned at Gabriel.

Lian walked directly behind Gabriel as they left the locker room area with the rest of their team. Lian's eyes were on the gold number eleven in bold stitch across the back of Gabriel's dark green jersey as they entered the large coliseum.

The academy spared no expense for this venue. Large pillars stood on each side of them as they entered the arena. An expanse of green grass chalked with white lines marked for the game stood in front of them. Lian was amazed at the rows of seats encircling them, expanding up so high he had to block the sun with his hand in order to see the last row. He continued to scan the top of the oval-shaped arena, and when his eyes reached the center section, he saw two large lion statues facing out toward the crowd. The huge cats seemed to loom over the stadium, symbolically marking their territory. A large Tri-Asterisk symbol embossed in a bronze relief faced out between the figures, and an enclosed rectangular sky box was tucked cozily underneath. Lian could not make out who was sitting inside, but he figured it had to be the headmasters from both schools and other dignitaries who graced the box.

Lian had still never even seen Headmaster Gorvant in the flesh. He was like a ghost figure whose presence was always felt, always watching, but never seen. On the portrait and holographic bust of the headmaster, there was a look in his eyes as though his stare could penetrate through whomever or whatever he gazed. With that in mind, Lian thought it was better he had not yet met Gorvant, although he was still curious about him.

Lian looked over as Gabriel nudged him. The other team was entering on the other side of the stadium. Their bright red uniforms stood in sharp contrast to the Tri-Asterisk dark green. Lian noticed his teammates were also curiously watching the Fair Gate players, who turned briefly to size up their competition as they walked to the other side of the field.

Once the players warmed up and went through their pre-game exercises, both teams returned to their respective benches. The referees gathered mid-field and began pointing at various parts of the playing field. The coaches walked back and forth in front of their benches of players, giving their last minute instructions and strategies for the game.

The school anthems started playing, and both teams stood watching the school's giant holograms swirling above the soccer field. The Fair Gate anthem was played first, and it was like any other anthem Lian had ever heard, including his own school song. During the Tri-Asterisk anthem, Lian viewed many people in the crowd making the same pyramid symbol over their chest like students did in the hallway. Suddenly the anthem ended, and Gorvant's voice rang through the stadium. "The Tri-Asterisk Eagles of America would like to welcome the Fair Gate Falcons of Great Britain in the first soccer match of the season."

Lian was suddenly feeling nervous about his first game. His thoughts were focused so much on other things it just occurred to him he had to perform. He had to quickly prepare himself mentally for the challenge ahead in this game. He reached inside his jersey and grasped the silver medallion on the necklace his mother had given him. He ran his thumb over the top. The feel of the metal always helped him feel more relaxed.

Lian's mind suddenly flashed back to his mom handing him a box.

"It's for protection." His mom studied his face carefully.

"Protection?" Lian wondered why he would ever need protection. When he looked up at her, a slight smile had spread across her face.

"And the Guardians rose from the depths to battle the Trinity." Lian continued to gaze at his mom as she spoke, her face becoming more serious. "Promise me you will always wear it, Lian."

He nodded his head.

"The Guardians," Lian said under his breath as he thought again of the figures in the fountain. He looked down at the circular shape and the engraved picture of a lady, her head bowed forward and eyes closed shut. The lady resembled his mother so closely he thought it was her when he first saw it eight years ago. Now he wondered if the lady was one of those figures. There had to be a link somewhere. He flipped it over and stared down at the image of a celestial body.

"Promise me you will always wear it, Lian." His mom's words echoed in his head.

The sounds of the game became more intense again around him. He flipped the medallion back over and lightly kissed the top. *For protection,* he thought as he walked with his team to the edge of the playing field.

Lian looked up at all the faces staring down at him and the other players. It suddenly felt strange for him to be playing as a representative for a school he didn't really know.

"Ready?" Gabriel saw the players beginning to take their places on the field.

Lian nodded at Gabriel as they got into position. He was playing left midfielder with Gabriel as the right forward. His heart was racing as the whistle blew again and the game was under way.

Three players from Fair Gate were running toward them once the ball was kicked into play. They quickly seized the ball at their feet as they ran downfield towards the Tri-Asterisk goal. At the halfway line Lian ran up the side, ready to protect the left, and tried to move in front and steal the ball from one of them as it was being passed. He lunged his foot forward and blocked the pass, while his other foot came up from behind and launched the ball towards midfield. The ball flew toward Gabriel who began dribbling it toward the Fair Gate goal. Lian ran forward to block the other team when someone suddenly hit him on the side of the jaw. A searing pain from the force of the blow made his head jolt to the side. As he went to the ground he grabbed his mouth, and the taste of blood ran over his tongue. His eyes were a little blurred as he turned his head to see who had hit him. One of the Fair Gate players was standing over him, staring down at him. His brown hair was cropped short with a V-like shape over his forehead, and his nostrils were flaring in and out slowly as he turned away.

Lian kept watching him as he jogged away, the number fifty-one on his back. More players ran past Lian quickly as he looked down at his hand speckled with blood. His eyes darted across the field as Gabriel passed the ball to the center striker. The ball blazed past the Fair Gate goalie and into the net. A loud horn blared, and the players took their places again.

Lian pulled himself up and went back to his midfielder spot, more determined than ever to keep playing. Gabriel was grinning as Lian gave him a thumbs-up for the great pass. He turned back around, and Player Fifty-one was now staring him down from across the field. It was strange, but Lian had the sense this player was out to get him.

The referee's whistle resonated again as play resumed. The ball was kicked to the right and then back to the center again, and Lian ran straight for Player Fifty-one, who was bearing down on the ball with the other players. Lian was so bent on revenge as he was running, he didn't notice the ball was headed for the Fair Gate goal. He side-stepped an oncoming player, his eyes dead-set on paying back Fifty-one. He was ready this time to elbow him in the side. As Lian approached him and his arm went up to deliver the blow, he looked his opponent right in his eyes. Lian instantly stopped and gasped as something changed quickly with Fifty-one's eyes. His pupils had transformed into slits for a mere second, and images of snakes instantly entered Lian's mind. He was caught so off-guard, he tripped on Fifty-one's foot and fell forward, landing face down. This time Lian felt Fifty-one's cleat collide hard into his already injured jaw as he ran off to join the play. Writhing in pain, Lian cradled his jaw as other players zoomed past him once more. A trumpet blared again, and this time the Fair Gate team roared at the sidelines. Even in agony, Lian realized he could have stopped that goal from happening had he paid attention to the play instead of taking care of his personal vendetta.

Lian got up slowly, and saw Coach Adams signaling for him with an angry look on his face. He knew he was being benched, and rightfully so. Lian thought about his father once again, and was relieved he was not at the game to witness his performance and behavior. He covered his jaw and moved slowly toward the sidelines. Gabriel caught sight of him getting an ice pack for his face, held his arms out, and mouthed "What happened?" Lian just shook his head and took his place on the bench, still tasting blood from the cut on his tongue and cheek. He looked over at the Fair Gate team, many of whom were still celebrating the goal. He felt a chill come over him as he thought of Player Fifty-one's eyes. The dark slits and the overall strength of the player bothered Lian. He'd never felt such strength from a single player in all of his years of playing soccer.

The game seemed to quickly progress, and before Lian realized it, the ice pack had warmed considerably, and the stadium's horn and the referee's whistle went off to signal half-time. Still on a high from the game, Gabriel ran up to Lian as the teams walked back to the locker rooms. He was deep into a personal celebration for his two assists and another goal he scored himself, and the Tri-Asterisk team was leading 3-2 at the half.

"Sorry you got benched, but great pass on the first goal." Gabriel's eyes widened as Lian turned around to face him, because his jaw was now swollen and dried blood was on his chin and down the front of his uniform. "What happened?"

"One of the Fair Gate players came straight at me. I didn't even see it coming." Lian grabbed a towel, wiped more blood off his face, and then threw the towel over the bench.

"I told you we have to watch out for that British team. You know, the way they train."

Lian realized Gabriel seemed to be trying to make light of the situation.

"The player that hit me...he was so strong, and he hit me so quickly and with such force." Lian shook his head as he spoke. "There was something else strange about him too. His eyes...I looked up and saw his eyes. They changed into slits. It all happened so quickly, maybe only for a second or two, but they looked like snake eyes or something." He glanced down at his hands as he tried to remember any other details. "I was so shocked, I lost my footing. I tripped, and then he kicked me in the jaw again. That's all I can remember. Besides being benched, that is."

"Do you know what you are saying? I mean, everything happens so quick out there on the field, you know? You sure it wasn't a glare or shadow around his eyes or something? You know...making it seem like they changed." Gabriel shifted his eyes back and forth, and seemed uncomfortable. He gently put his hand on Lian's chin and turned his head so he could get a better look at his bruised jaw. "And looking at your face now, he must have kicked you pretty hard." Gabriel paused for a second, and continued as he pulled his own head back. "Wait a minute. You're telling me he kicked you twice?" Gabriel looked closer at his swollen jaw. "Well, I didn't see that one. So, that's all the more reason I'm saying maybe you were just seeing things. I know I would have seen stars."

"No. No, that's not it." Lian shook his head methodically. "You're not listening to what I'm saying."

"Look. You had your cage rattled good, and not once, but twice. Lian, you were shook up."

"Don't believe me then." Lian turned his back to Gabriel as he grabbed another jersey out of his locker and made his way to the sinks to wash his face.

"I didn't say I didn't believe you. I'm just wondering if there is another explanation is all."

Lian was tired of trying to convince Gabriel of what happened. He felt his best friend should just believe him, with no doubts and no questions asked. His eyes flashed with anger as he thought about the whole ordeal with Player Fifty-one. Lian could feel the anger building as Gabriel was talking-his words were barely an echo in the back of his head, but still registering enough to inflame the trembling rage now coursing through his body.

"The ref should have seen that too, and he should at least have given that guy a yellow card." Gabriel continued, shaking his head slowly back and forth.

Lian stood next to the lockers wearing a strange intense look on his face...his normally soft features more angular, his brows knitted together, while his eyes were almost glazed over. Standing with his shoulders curled forward in a semi-hunched position, he was larger than normal and his long muscles bulked up and huge.

"Lian?" he whispered. No answer. "Lian." Gabriel whispered louder, waving his hands in front of his face. A few of the other players turned to look at Gabriel, but Lian continued to stare off into the distance. Suddenly Lian turned back around and quickly stormed out of the locker room. Gabriel jumped up to follow, but Lian's gait of long strides was so quick, he had to run to catch up.

"Hey, Lian." he barely snagged the back of Lian's shirt before they were on the field.

Lian did not break stride or turn around as his arm pushed him aside in one large sweeping motion. Gabriel flew backwards a few feet and landed with a thud on the ground. "Leave me alone." growled Lian, his voice deeper, almost animalistic.

"What the heck?" Gabriel now knew something was really wrong. He watched Lian disappear around the corner, and tried to stand up as the rest of the team all passed by. Gabriel hissed as some of them bumped into him, stepped and tripped on his feet, and practically ran over him without a second glance. "Thanks for the hand."

Everyone was nearly in position by the time Gabriel took his place on the field. His eyes immediately shot over to Lian, still hunched forward. He was now aiming that aggression toward the other team. He still appeared oblivious to not only what just transpired, but everything else except the opponent right in front of him.

"I don't believe this." Gabriel looked back at Lian. A split-second after the whistle sounded, he watched as Lian flew past him, moving so fast and with such speed he almost seemed like a blur. Gabriel and the other players had hardly budged, but his eyes widened as he saw Lian suddenly leap astonishingly high in the air and come down on top of Player Fifty-one across the field.

All action stopped before it had a chance to begin as the attention shifted on the two opponents. Lian jumped to his feet, the bottom of his cleat now pressed against Fifty-one's throat, his opponent's eyes bulging out as the rest of his face matched the color of his jersey. Gabriel's head shot back toward the referee who was running over to the skirmish.

"Call it." Gabriel yelled as he closed in on the two players. "Blow the whistle." He reached the scene just as Lian's foot released its stranglehold, and his arm jetted back in the air behind him to strike. "Noooo." Gabriel screamed as the referee blew his whistle.

Gabriel leaped forward and caught Lian's arm as it started plummeting toward the player's face. He tightened his grip as he was flung effortlessly downward like an extension of Lian's arm, lifted back up again, and then hurled down once more to bounce off Fifty-one's body. With Gabriel removed from his arm, Lian's fist came down and hit the ground right next to the player's face with a heavy thud. Gabriel let out a gasp as he ran back and clutched mercilessly onto Lian's arm again. This time the arm did not move, and Lian, totally exhausted, fell to his knees.

Gabriel panted heavily for a few seconds, "Are we done?" feeling the wind nearly knocked out of him.

Lian grunted and stared back at Gabriel who finally released his arm. The referee had arrived shouting, "Get off of him. Give him some room to breathe." as he kneeled down to check on Fifty-one, who lay nearly unconscious on the field.

"It's all right buddy. Come on." Gabriel coaxed in a calm even tone as he rose and helped Lian stand and led him away. Glancing left and right as players from both teams stared at them, Gabriel headed for the bench, his arm around the shoulders of a trembling Lian. When he reached the sidelines, he turned Lian around, helped him sit on the bench, and headed back to the field.

The referee signaled the Fair Gate bench for the coach and trainer, and held up a red card as he pointed at Lian. He put the red card in his pocket, and pulled out a yellow card, this time pointing at Gabriel.

"Me? I didn't do anything. I tried to break it up." Gabriel ran quickly toward the official.

"Get your buddy and head for the showers." Coach Adams stopped Gabriel from going any further. "He's done, and they gave you ten minutes."

Gabriel hung his head, and then looked over at Lian who still seemed to be out of it. Gabriel walked over, grabbed hold of his friend's arm, relieved when he recognized the look about him was one of total exhaustion. The concern Lian could change again and run back out on the field disappeared quickly. It was a side of Lian he'd never seen before and was still struggling to understand. Inside the locker room, he released Lian's arm as he sat him down on the bench by their lockers. His face was pale with a blank expression, and his eyes had dark rings under them as if he had not slept in days. Lian Hunter was absolutely spent.

"Here, drink this." Gabriel placed a sports bottle of cold water in his hand. Lian held it loosely, and with his hands still weak and trembling, he dropped it. Gabriel scooped up the bottle, and knelt down in front of him. "Let's try that again." He held it right in front of Lian, this time allowing him to grasp the container himself. Lian took a sip of water, cradled the sports bottle near his chest, and stared straight ahead.

Gabriel moved in close so he was inches away from Lian's face. "Are you okay?" he voiced with a ring of deep concern.

Lian blinked slowly twice, and then kept his eyes closed. He inhaled a deep guttural breath, took another sip, and nodded his head.

"Man, Lian. What the heck happened to you?" Gabriel sat flat on the floor, crossed his legs, and looked up at Lian, watching every muscle in his face.

"I don't know." Lian strained to take a breath. He cleared his throat and opened his eyes. "I must have blacked out or something."

"I'd say. You almost buried that guy in the ground," his voice nearly an octave higher.

Lian took another small sip of water and returned to staring forward over Gabriel's head, shaking his head slowly. "I just...just felt like I lost myself."

"Yeah, I could tell." He slowly pointed at Lian, "You seemed...well, different, like you'd become someone else."

Lian thought for a second, "I don't know. I don't know what happened. What I do know I was really ticked, and I just couldn't let that guy get away with kicking me like that."

Gabriel let out a small laugh. "Well, if it makes you feel any better, I don't think he'll ever mess with you again. Not with *that* attack." moving his hand up in the air and smacking it down on his other hand, trying to imitate Lian's initial assault.

Lian shook his head in agreement, but remained solemn and expressionless. He could not remember anything but the anger swelling up in him.

Gabriel stood up, "I got to get back out there. My ten minutes are almost up." He gave Lian a comforting hand on his shoulder, "Are you going to be okay?"

"Yeah...yeah, I'm fine now, Gabe."

"Take a nice long shower and you'll feel better."

"I will. And thanks." Lian assured Gabriel on his way back out onto the field.

As Lian got ready for his shower, he was in heavy thought. This angst was a part of him he'd never felt before. Why could he not remember how this happened? It scared him to feel that far out of control. His memory revealed only two things. First, that the whole incident seemed like a dream or more precisely, a nightmare from which he couldn't wake up. And secondly, that he recalled reality returning as he was kneeling over the other player, wondering how he got there.

As the water ran over his head, Lian's thoughts shifted to his family, and how nice it would be to feel wrapped in the safety and comfort of home. His mind quickly shifted again back to Gabriel's remark, "You seemed different, like you'd become someone else." He thought for a second, and then confessed quietly.

"I was someone else."

Chapter Eight

The Lost Cave

Saturday morning came through Lian's window along with the sound of Gabriel's four-wheeler pulling into the yard. Lian got out of bed, went to the window just in time to see his best friend walking toward his backdoor. He quickly got dressed, brushed his teeth, and headed downstairs. Gabriel was sitting in front of a huge plate of scrambled eggs and some sort of small fish laid out in a row as Lian's mom was pouring a glass of orange juice for him.

"Good morning," greeted Lian.

"Good morning, hon." His mother had a big smile, as Gabriel looked up and grinned as much as he could with a mouthful of eggs. "You want some eggs too…maybe some kippers?"

Lian looked at the fish with their heads and tails still on, their eyes looking up at him. It suddenly reminded him of the reptile embryo staring up at him in Professor Snodgrass class. "Just eggs please. How are you doing this morning, pal?"

Gabriel shook his head as he finished up chewing his food. "Just got up, huh?"

"Yeah, I probably would have slept in a little more, but I heard the sound of someone's four-wheeler outside my window and it woke me up."

"Well, you said bright and early."

"Yeah, and I guess this does qualify as bright and early." Lian grinned and took a drink of orange juice.

Both boys quickly finished up their breakfast, and headed outside.

"I'll bring mine around." Lian went into his garage to fetch his four-wheeler.

Gabriel started his vehicle, and they both headed down the road toward the beach. They stayed on the road most of the way, but had to give way to two cars coming up behind them. When they reached the beach entrance, they cut their wheels sharply to the right, and headed down the path of dirt and sand leading straight to the beach area. They both loved the feeling of bouncing up and down on the contours of the sand as they flew along just out of the reach of the tide.

After riding along the shore for a while, they headed for their secret hide-out, "The Lost Cave," as they called it. The name always gave each of them a special feeling, and just had an aura of mystery about it. This was most likely because of the "Lost" part of the name, like they were the only ones who found it. It was a difficult location to spot, unless one would be very close to the entrance and look very long and hard at how to enter it. The entryway itself angled slightly off to the right, and the huge rock at the entrance gave off an optical illusion there was no opening at all. It was inset at just the right angle that unless you knew there was an opening right to its right, one would never see it.

How Lian and Gabriel ever found their cave was very much by accident. They were playing a hide and seek game about the cave around five years earlier. Lian was trying to find a place to hide, and noticed the inset rock. As Gabriel was moving toward him and getting close enough to spot him, Lian moved to the left to squeeze into what he thought was a small crevice, but no crevice was there. He felt nothing there to stop him from going farther, so he carefully slid to his left with his back touching the rock the entire time. Lian thought with every inch he traveled he would eventually run into and be stopped by a rock.

About five feet into the crevice he realized the rock supporting his back started to curve around and head deeper into the wall. He kept his back tightly against the rock until he saw the passageway opened up into a bigger and much brighter area. "It's a cave." Lian stood there motionless, astonished at his find. He began to move around and take in the walls, the floor, and the huge V-shaped rock ceiling looming above him. As he turned around, Lian noticed the light was coming from the huge rock behind him, the same rock whose other side supported his back as he traveled the passageway just moments earlier. He found himself completely amazed at the rock standing before him...from inside one could see right through this big rock and outside the cave, like a one-way mirror. He ran out and called for Gabriel.

Gabriel moved slowly inside the opening and could do nothing more than stare in awe at the surroundings as Lian showed him the rest of his discovery.

"And look at that." Gabriel pointed at the opening of the cave through the huge one-way mirror rock.

"I know. I saw that. How is that even possible, Gabe? It's a rock."

"I'll have to research this, but I think it is like a one-way mirror. A mirror can be made from a lot of things, but today they are basically glass with a really thin layer of silvered metal. The glass is made of sand, but the reflective surface is a shiny metal, mostly aluminum today."

Gabriel paused for a few seconds, looked closer at the rock, and then continued as Lian listened attentively. "Actually, the first mirrors were purely natural reflections you know...pools of water. The first man-made mirrors were made out of obsidian, a type of volcanic rock."

"Hmmm...so what do you think this rock is made of?" Lian watched his friend carefully.

Gabriel started to massage his chin with his index finger and thumb. "Well, with one-way mirrors like we seem to have here, the lighter side reflects and the darker side is basically hidden. But somehow the other side doesn't reflect, or we would have seen ourselves, you know? And we didn't, did we? So...as far as what this rock is made of...I am not certain. Like I said, I will have to look it up. I mean, maybe this big rock is really just a big piece of sand."

"Yeah, maybe. This is so great. We've got to tell somebody about this."

Gabriel quickly put his hand on his best friend's shoulder. "Lian...I don't think we should tell *anyone* about this. This should be our secret. We are the ones who found it, and that was very much by sheer luck, because the entrance is so hidden-basically lost within the rocks`."

Lian thought for a couple seconds, "You're right, Gabe. No one needs to know about this…except us. We may need this as a hiding place someday. It could be our secret meeting place if we are ever in trouble or something."

"Exactly. I wonder how far it goes back. It seems to have a bunch of twists and turns in it, you could get lost in it."

"Well, the key word I keep hearing about this place is "lost," so why don't we call it the "Lost Cave" – *our* "Lost Cave"."

"That's good, Lian."

"At some point it has to either dead end or open up somewhere else. Do you think the thing goes back pretty far?"

"I don't know. Maybe we can explore the rest of it later." Gabriel stretched his neck out and looked as far down the back of the cave as he could manage.

They perused the main area, which was spacious and contained many rocks of all different sizes and shapes. They started setting up a sitting area using some of the more squared-off rocks as seats and a couple others as a small table. Both boys closely examined the ceiling and the surrounding walls.

Lian noticed some strange writing and pictures with stick figures and other primitive drawings on the wall to the far right.

"Gabe. Come here…it looks like we're not the first ones to use this cave."

Gabriel hustled over. "Hmmm…looks like some kids were in here before, that's for sure."

"I'm not so sure it was kids though. Maybe…because of the drawings, but look at this writing...that doesn't look like something kids would do, does it?"

"No, not really." Gabriel went back and forth between studying the writing and then looking back at the pictures. "I've read about this kind of thing before."

"Really?"

"Yeah…it's weird, because I just read something about Chumash rock art and the Chumash people who lived in this area a long time ago. I seem to remember they did something like this with the pictures, but nothing I read mentioned any writing to go along with it. Egyptian and Sumerian hieroglyphics used these types of symbols with this style of writing, but why they would be here is a mystery. I'll have to look it up again later."

"Well, it's weird, whatever it is."

As they left their cave they looked around for some kind of marker reminding them where the cave entrance was. The walls there were so similar in nature up and down the beach.

"It's right below that tree on the bluffs. And that's the last tree before the bluffs cut back a bit. Do you see that?" Lian raised his hand, his finger zeroing in on the lonely tree.

"Yeah, that's good. Remember that, or it could really be our Lost Cave."

Chapter Nine

ROTC

As Lian and Gabriel were walking to their next class, Lian noticed a man in dark green military fatigues walking through the crowd. The beret on his head was cocked forward to the left and dark green as well with a patch on the front. He towered over most of the students as he made his way down the hall, and his face carried a deadpan expression. His eyes darted back and forth slowly at the oncoming students, seemingly scanning each of them as they passed, as if weighing his options, deciding which students could make the grade in the military.

When he got closer, Lian recognized him as the man he saw a couple weeks earlier, although then he had on a blue uniform with a thin flight cap. A table was set up further down the corridor with two more military officers in their dress blue uniforms sitting behind it, and some upperclassmen waiting in line to talk to them.

As they were walking past the soldier in fatigues, he put his arm out, hitting Lian in the chest with his hand. A badge on his pocket read "ROTC Recruiter," and as Lian looked up from his shirt, the man was staring deep into Lian's eyes, and completely ignoring Gabriel, whose hand was out to get a pamphlet as well. After a moment the soldier clicked his feet, his whole body turned quickly and stiffly to the right, and he walked off in a march-like cadence.

Lian looked over at Gabriel. "What was that about?"

Gabriel turned and watched the soldier walk away. They both

looked down and examined the pamphlet which had a picture on the front of three military officers in a triangular formation and a blue circle with wings that said "We want you. Join ROTC today."

Lian shrugged his shoulders and opened the pamphlet, which showed a large facility and more photos of soldiers carrying guns in a V-shaped alignment. The "We Want You" slogan was in big bold print on the inside as well.

"We Want You?" Gabriel read again as Lian started to laugh. "I guess they didn't want me."

Chapter Ten

Indigo?

"Don't you agree?" Gabriel was talking to Lian, but his words were like background noise drifting in and out.

"Yeah...sure." Lian turned his head only halfway toward Gabriel, but his entire focus was on Annaka who was now gliding toward him in slow motion. Her dark eyes were fixated on his and held them like a magnet. He could feel himself breathing harder, his chest heaving in and out. He swallowed, and could tell his mouth was becoming drier by the second. Annaka brought out something animalistic in him. Her pale white skin was a stark contrast to her jet black hair that fell like an impenetrable shield past her shoulders. Her features were sharp, the antithesis of delicate. There was nothing ethereal about Annaka Dimortra.

Lian was taken aback when Annaka suddenly wedged herself between them. She was now facing him and standing so close he felt his personal space was being invaded, yet he didn't care. Her scent was even a contradiction-musky, yet floral, and making him feel even more intoxicated by her, as if that was possible.

"Don't you want to ask me?" Annaka's tone made it sound like more of a demand than a question. She had the same unnerving grin on her face to which Lian was becoming accustomed, and in fact, beginning to like.

"Ask you what?" Lian responded after a brief pause.

"The *dance*?" Annaka added a quick and slight left-to-right shake of her head.

Lian stood dumbfounded. He hadn't even paid attention to all the posters hanging in the academy corridors or the daily announcements given over the intercom. He had been so wrapped up in his own thoughts. He looked down at Annaka, whose arms were now crossed over her chest, and thought it best to say something.

"Of course, the *dance*...yeah, alright." It happened so quickly, Lian did not realize he gave a response. A dead silence hung in the air as he stood there transfixed on her eyes, which suddenly widened. Lian could feel the blood rushing to his face as it finally dawned on him.

"Oh...you want to go to the..." Lian could feel the pressure of everyone's eyes on him. He cleared his throat and started again. "I mean, will you go to the dance with me?" he let out a deep breath, relieved to get the words out.

"I'll think about it." Annaka grinned with a glint in her eyes as she shoved a folded piece of paper into his hand. She turned in a swift motion, her hair brushing Lian's face and then fanning out around her as she glided away.

Lian brought his hand up to his face to feel where Annaka's hair grazed him, and watched with Gabriel as she walked away to rejoin her group of friends. The other girls were all staring over at them as Annaka moved into the center of the group, and turned around to stare as well. Her academy uniform fit her tightly, different than the other girls. Her blue and green plaid skirt seemed a little shorter and her white button up shirt seemed to be straining under pressure.

Gabriel turned to Lian, "Where did that come from?"

Lian just shook his head as he unfolded the note she had given him:

7:30 P.M.
5809 Willow Gate
Dress color: Indigo
Make sure to coordinate your tux

Something fell out of the note. Lian bent down to pick it up and realized it was a piece of fabric. He held it up between his thumb and index finger and let it hang like it was a bug. The color was so vague he could not tell if it was blue or purple. He looked over at Gabriel who was laughing.

"Indigo?"

Chapter Eleven

Charlemagne

Charlemagne was the name of the main hangout for most of the students at Tri-Asterisk Academy. Here every student could intermingle with other students regardless of their grade, although everyone still seemed to stick to their own small cliques and grade level.

Upon entering Charlemagne, one would notice candles inside ornately decorated brass lamps hanging from the fifteen-foot ceilings were basically the only source of light. Sand colored Greek-styled columns around the edges of the room stood in direct contrast against the dark red walls. A series of Persian rugs butted up against one another across the entire floor holding four-foot-high rectangular wooden tables with tall stools. Large pillow-like booths weaved with vivid colors were spread along the perimeter of the room. The aroma of many different types of food streamed through the air, usually creating appetites for many of the students. In the back of the hangout was a game room. Although some of the games were of the older classic types, including pinball machines, most of them were holographic in nature, which gave an authentic virtual reality feel to them. The game room was a very popular feature of Charlemagne, usually filled with customers lined up waiting to play the various games.

The sound of the most popular music filled the air. Each table could choose a theme for the entire establishment, and even though the whole décor would not change, it would appear to do so from each table's perspective. For instance, one could choose a desert oasis atmosphere, or a retro look, like having a polka-dot floor and jukeboxes placed in every booth like the old time soda shops that allowed patrons to choose their favorite songs to be played throughout the shop right at their table. Everyone enjoyed this particular feature too, and together with the game room, it made Charlemagne a unique establishment with a very relaxing and entertaining atmosphere. It was such a great place to unwind for many students, especially the ones who felt the full weight of the heavy load of classes at the Academy.

Lian, Jimmy, and Gabriel walked into Charlemagne right after school, and once their eyes adjusted to the darkness, they sat down at one of the tables near the corner of the room. A holographic image of a computer screen appeared on the table as they sat down. The screen displayed a variety of theme selections. "How about a nature theme today?" Jimmy pushed the "Nature Setting" button, and the boys were instantly surrounded by greenery, beautiful trees and shrubs ornate with flowers, a waterfall and babbling brook running right up to and surrounding their table. A young waiter approached them from a path in between the trees wearing a blue collared shirt that read "Charlemagne" in the upper left corner. A patch on his right arm showed a picture of a bearded man wearing a crown.

"Good afternoon. My name is Dane, and I will take your drink orders first. So what can I get you, gentlemen? I do want to mention we have a special going on with each of our various berry presses…half-price until six o'clock." The waiter passed out the brilliantly colored laminated menus, one sheet with food and drink choices printed on both sides.

"I think the special sounds good to me." Lian looked around at the other two for their reactions. He thought back to his mom's crepes, "Could I get a lingonberry press?"

"Lingonberry? You got me on that one." Dane grabbed one of the menus on the table and pointed out the drink and flavor selections. "I'm sorry, we don't have that particular one. Our available flavors are listed on the back here."

"Ha-ha…that's exactly what *I* said." Lian quipped as Dane's face assumed a quizzical expression. "Never mind. Ummm...I will just take a blueberry then."

"One blueberry." The waiter paused and waited for the other two boys to speak.

Jimmy shook his head back and forth, "I don't know...I don't know."

Gabriel put down his menu, "Well, I will have one of those as well."

"Okay. Another blueberry it is. Sir?"

Jimmy moved his finger across the flavors on the menu, "Oh, I don't know. Just bring me an orange one. That'd be fine."

"Okay, that will be three presses, two blueberry and one orange. Will that be all?" the waiter checked.

"That's it. Thank you," Lian replied.

"Thank *you*. I'll be back to take your food orders when I bring your drinks." Dane walked off through the trees and toward the kitchen.

"You know, I've never tried the orange, but I bet it will be good, Jimmy." Gabriel looked over the food on the menu. "Are you guys hungry, or are we just going to get drinks?"

"Just drinks for me. I'm not that hungry at all." Lian put his menu on the table, stretched his arms, and leaned back into the cushiony chair.

Jimmy shook his head, "Yeah, just drinks are fine."

The waiter returned with their drinks, and asked for their food order.

"I think we are just going to stick to drinks at this point, Dane." Lian collected the menus and placed them at the corner of the table.

"Very well... I'll be back to check on you later. Enjoy."

"Thank you."

"What a nice serene setting you picked, Jimmy...very peaceful. I like it." Lian looked around at all the color surrounding their table.

"Has Professor Cordovak's class been getting easier for you, James?" Gabriel shifted in his seat and turned towards the other two.

"No, not really. I can't come up with a project she likes or will approve for her class. I'm pretty sure she doesn't like me."

"It's not you, Jimmy. She doesn't like anyone." Lian put his hand on Jimmy's shoulder trying to comfort him.

"She seems to like you." Jimmy took a long sip of his press.

"She tolerates me, but that's far from liking me. You know, she's gotten on me a little bit before too…you just weren't there to see it."

"Her toleration for you isn't the same as her dislike for me."

"Well, at least let us help you get a project topic she *will* approve." Gabriel put his index finger up to his lips and looked up in thought. "Let's see. How about doing it on electro-magnetism? That's such a big topic, so you should be able to find a subcategory you can use. If you don't like that, maybe you could try using antimatter?"

"Hmmm…electro-magnetism seems pretty good. What are some subcategories?"

"Well…there is the principle of force, and fields of magnetism, static electricity, lightning, and many others."

"Lightning. Lightning sounds good. I think that would be pretty interesting to do."

"And I *know* that Cordovak will approve it, as long as no one else in one of her classes has picked it first."

The waiter arrived once again through the scenery. "How are we doing here? Anything else I can get you now? Another press?"

"No, not yet. I think we're fine for a while. But thanks." Gabriel responded.

"Alright, I will check back with you later. If you don't want anything else, you can just pay the bill here whenever you're ready."

"Thanks again."

"Let's go to the game room." Lian pointed both index fingers towards that area.

They got up and walked through the shrubbery into the game room area. The lines had gone down substantially, and they immediately got to one of the game stations called Battle Zones.

"Any particular ideas on a zone today?"

"I never tried the caves, if that is okay with you guys."

"Yeah, sure. The caverns it is."

Jimmy touched the buttons to select three players in the caverns scenario, and they were instantly standing in a very dark cave with passages in almost every direction. Three laser type weapons were flashing in permanent holsters under the game console right in front of them.

"This is so great." Jimmy picked up one of the guns. He changed his voice to a soft gravelly tone to sound like a rough and tough military commander, "Let's go find the enemy, boys…maybe do a little damage."

Lian and Gabriel grabbed their weapons and headed down one of the passageways with Jimmy. As they made the turn around the first curve, something dark jumped out from the shadows and took aim right at Lian. Gabriel quickly raised his laser toward the target, and with a bright beam of light and a loud electronic zapping noise, the approaching figure went down. Gabriel went over to examine the fallen enemy soldier, but before he could get there, it flashed dimly a few times and disappeared.

"Good shot, Gabe." Lian moved forward. "Hey, there's an opening up ahead."

They walked slowly in a triad formation, watching out for any enemy soldiers who may want to ambush them. The tunnel opened up into a large mountainous area.

"There are two of them up there on the left, right behind that big rock. You guys see 'em?" Gabriel whispered.

"I'm going to go around to the far left and try to get them from the side." Jimmy took two steps and his weapon glowed brightly twice, and shut down, indicating he was shot by the enemy. "Awww…I'm hit, guys. You got to finish these two off for me."

Gabriel and Lian crouched low and headed for the two snipers up in the rocks. When they arrived far below the ledge where the enemy soldiers were positioned, Gabriel signaled they split up and go at the snipers" spot from both directions. Lian went to the right, Gabriel to the left, both carefully climbing the mountain's paths as quietly as possible. As Lian approached the targets, two shots rang out.

"Got 'em both, Lian."

"Great work, Gabe." Lian was just in time to see the snipers disappear. Suddenly, he picked up the sound of small rocks falling from below and footsteps of someone approaching. He threw his back against the rock and aimed his weapon downward towards the sound.

"I'm back in the game, fellas." Jimmy announced as his head crested the ledge below Lian. "Thanks for ridding us of those two. I hate waiting those two minutes to get the power back to your weapon."

"Hey, I almost shot you."

"You gotta be more careful, Jimmy." Gabriel approached flipping a switch on his laser to reload. "I say we divide and conquer from here out." Gabriel scanned the terrain above them. "Jimmy, go straight up, Lian, right, and I'll head left, and let's meet at the top."

"This is so great, isn't it? I forgot how much fun this game is." Jimmy shook his head as he looked up at his destination.

"Yes, it is. Alright...we've taken care of three of these guys, which leaves nine enemy soldiers left in our Dirty Dozen game." Lian checked back and forth between Jimmy and Gabriel.

"Let's move out, and we'll get the final count when we meet at the summit." Gabriel moved his weapon up into the ready position and headed left.

"See ya at the top, comrades." Jimmy headed up the big rock in front of him, and Lian found an easy path to the right.

Along the way Lian heard the familiar zapping sounds of weapons discharging to his left, and thought about Gabriel and Jimmy encountering enemy soldiers as they made their way up the mountain. Again his ears picked up a rustling of sliding rocks to his left, and he caught a glimpse of a helmet moving slowly behind a large boulder. Aiming his laser at the end of the large rock, he fired as soon as his holographic foe appeared from behind his cover. The figure fell forward as the ray hit him dead center in the chest, and his rifle went flying from his hands. Lian hustled over toward the soldier lying face down on the ground just in time to see him vanish.

"Another one bites the dust." Lian made his way around the boulder and up toward the crest. He had just gone a few yards when another enemy soldier quickly jumped out from behind a vertical standing rock, and fired toward him. The shot just barely missed Lian, as he dove to his right for cover. That dive knocked the breath out of him, and as he was trying to catch it, he heard the holographic figure slowly approaching. He silently turned onto his back and listened intensely to try and pinpoint his enemy's exact location. He then raised and aimed his laser at the spot from where he thought the soldier would emerge. As if on cue, the figure appeared and Lian shot first. The soldier fell hard and landed on the ground right next to Lian. As he was pulling himself from the ground, Lian looked at the image. This was not a humanoid face staring lifelessly back at Lian, but a green frightening-looking head of some creature that made Lian quickly scamper back and grip the rock next to him. As he was trying to study what was lying right in front of him, the weird features from this horrid image suddenly faded out and disappeared completely. Lian's body froze, but his mind was racing. He knew he had seen that head before. Even though its familiarity rang a bell inside his brain, he couldn't recall exactly where he'd previously seen it. He sat on the rock, his brain trying to uncover some clues to this new mystery. Lian heard the sound of the game's laser weapons going off in the distance, but he was in such deep thought none of those noises were really registering.

"Lian." Gabriel paused as he approached his friend from above. "Lian." Gabriel called as he shook Lian by the shoulder to stir him back into reality. "You okay?"

"Yeah." Lian was startled by Gabriel's touch. "Yeah...I'm fine." Lian stood up quickly and turned to face his companions. "What's going on? Did we get 'em all?"

"I don't know...Jimmy and I got seven of them, which leaves only two, which I assume you took care of."

"Yep, I got two."

"Good. Well, let's head down. I'm kind of thirsty again."

"Okay." Lian followed the other two as they moved down the paths between the rocks. "Hey...just wondering, but did either of you get a close look at those guys before they vanished?"

"Mine were too far away, and they were gone before I could

actually see them." Jimmy hunched up his shoulders.

"Yeah, I did. I saw one of them." Gabriel looked back at Lian. "Why do you ask?"

"I'm just wondering. Did they look normal to you?"

"Normal? You mean like *normal* - two arms, two legs, and the way a holographic soldier with dirt on his face and grease paint under his eyes would look? That kind of normal?"

"Yeah. I mean...he looked like us, right? Like human?"

"Well, his face looked like he was in pain, like he was supposed to look in that kind of situation, but yeah...human." Gabriel stopped walking, and turned completely around so he could look Lian in the eye. "Why? What are you getting at with this "human" stuff?"

"Well, I can't tell if I just imagined this or not, but the last one I shot fell down beside me, and I got a really good look at its face, and it was *not* human."

"Not human?" Jimmy was also staring at Lian's face. "What do you mean?"

Lian took a deep breath and continued, "It was green, for one thing. And it was a creature, definitely not human. More like a dinosaur's head...that was the first thing I thought of...like a reptile of some sort. I don't know...it's just so hard to describe, because it was there, and then it wasn't. I kept thinking I must be seeing things, but there it was. And then, it just faded away like the other ones."

"Now *that* is weird. A dinosaur head?" Jimmy's hand went to his forehead to scratch his brow as he sat down on a nearby rock.

"It's strange alright. But Lian, if you saw this thing, if you are sure you saw it, I wouldn't be so quick to dismiss it as just your imagination. Although it might be just that, there may be some kind of rational explanation for this. Something's going on here."

"The thing is, Gabe...I've seen this thing before, but I can't remember where or when." Lian looked at Gabriel as if he could provide the answer.

"It will come to you in time." Gabriel assured. "Right now, I'd just forget about it. Try to get it out of your mind, and just have some fun."

"Yeah, and then when you least expect it, it'll pop up somewhere in your brain. You'll remember it."

Gabriel affirmatively shook his head at Jimmy. "Let's go back to the table, get another drink. What do you say?"

Lian nodded and the three headed down the mountain and returned through the caverns to the main floor. They each placed their laser weapons into the holsters, and the cavern scene transformed back into the game room.

Back at the table, the three ordered another drink, talked more about the lightning idea for Jimmy, and discussed some of their classes and other students. Lian touched the computerized bill displayed on the table, added a tip to the total and pushed his thumb on the "Pay" tab.

"I got this today. And Gabe, I'm ready to head home."

"I'm ready too. I have some reading to catch up on. Call me if you need more help on your project idea, Jimmy."

"Okay, thanks, Gabriella. See you, Lian."

"Take care."

As Lian and Gabriel started to work their way out through the trees, the theme changed back so quickly into its original state and music simultaneously started playing again throughout the room, that it startled both of them. In perfect synchronization, they slowly turned their heads back to the table to see Jimmy grinning at them.

"Oops. A little slow on the metamorphosis for you, wasn't I?"

"No problem, Jimmy. We'll see you later."

Gabriel and Lian walked out of Charlemagne into the bright sunlight and got into the car.

"Fila, take us home, please. Gabriel will be the first stop." Lian watched his seatbelt fasten.

"Gabriel Stratus residence, forty point seven minutes, ETA 5:12P.M." Fila responded quickly as the car headed home.

"I'm just glad we didn't run into Annaka and her friends today, because they come here a lot. That would have been less than unpleasant." Lian frowned and looked at his friend.

"You're still thinking about her quite a bit, aren't you?"

"When I think about her good qualities, you know, the things I really like about her…those are always overshadowed by her other assets, the really *weird* ones." Lian started gazing out the window. "At least I am *trying* not to think about her too much anymore."

Lian turned to look at Gabriel, and then back once again to the sights outside his window. He thought about the creature again, but then quickly turned his mind's attention back to Annaka, and how she could always draw him in toward her…so effortlessly. He sat still, closed his eyes, and thought about the beauty in her eyes, her hair, her smile.

Chapter Twelve

The Museum

"Pretty cool we get out of class for half a day." Gabriel and Lian walked through the large doors of the Natural History Museum.

"Yeah, this must be Snodgrass's favorite hangout."

Looking at the long glass cases full of fossils, Lian noticed a musty smell permeating the air. Surveying the large empty room, he thought the museum would have been packed full of tourists, but his class seemed to be the only visitors here. He turned his head toward Snodgrass when he heard the professor's voice.

Snodgrass was talking to an elderly docent who was hunched over behind the counter. The man had sparse sprigs of white hair that looked out of place on his mostly bald head. His thin skin gave the illusion his bones were almost protruding out of it, and Lian thought the man looked as old as some of the artifacts.

"Right this way, class," ordered Professor Snodgrass as he walked from the information counter into another entryway.

Lian looked at the various displays of animals so lifelike through the mastery of taxidermy. It gave him a weird feeling to see the animals staring out through glass eyes, forever frozen in a mock environment of plastic plants and resin mirrored water.

"Here we are." Snodgrass cleared his throat. "As you can see, we are now in front of 'The City of Atlantis,' one of our nine wonders as you will recall."

Lian turned his focus to the large display in front him. Enormous white columns and small steps lined the front of a building. The way the display used an expansive white set against a light blue sky backdrop automatically gave Lian a very serene feeling. It looked like a beautiful place to live...everything seemed so tranquil.

"Although portions of the land are still being excavated near Bimini, we have been able to paint quite a clear picture of what life must have been like in this wondrous city."

Lian looked at all of the human-like figures wearing white robes in various poses. One of the figures near the front was a man with red hair who looked to be twelve feet tall. He was holding a strange looking instrument in one hand, while his other hand stretched out in front of him making some sort of gesture to a normal sized man.

The professor placed his hands on the copper-looking rail in front of him. "It's really something to see all the different types of people in this world who co-existed together peacefully. There is much we can learn from them today."

At first Lian thought the third figure in the group was a boy, but realized after looking closer it was a very small man, laden with wrinkles. All of the figures looked so real, as if they would talk or start moving at any minute.

"Any questions?" Snodgrass turned back to the class.

"Professor, what animal is that?" a student was pointing at an animal next to a wooden fence in the scenery, its body covered in thick and bushy white fur. This animal's head was down as if it was grazing on the green plastic grass of this make-believe meadow.

"Ah...well, that my young protégés, is what we call a sheep, or *ovis aries*, their species name in Latin, of course." Professor Snodgrass moved to the front of the display and studied it. "Sheep at one time were very common, and a very useful animal to humans. As food, we called their meat 'mutton.' The meat of that baby right there next to it, called a 'lamb' from birth until a year old, was especially tender, and therefore more popular and more in demand for culinary purposes. See how thick that fur is? That was known as 'wool,' and was at one time one of the most widely used fabrics for people. It would be sheared from the animal and then mass produced to be used for various types of clothing."

The students began discussing and talking among themselves, pointing and staring at the mock sheep, while some of the girls were fascinated with the endearing qualities of the lamb.

Snodgrass looked up and patted his chest a couple times. "That is until the Thylacine, or um...the 'Tasmanian Tiger,' as most of you call it, was widely reintroduced from extinction." Snodgrass looked over the top of his eyeglasses. "Survival of the fittest, my friends. Yes, I'm afraid there is always a price to pay when one decides to start tinkering around with nature. In this case, as one species was brought back from extinction, another species raced into it. Hardly a fair exchange."

"Did you check out the size of some of those people who lived in Atlantis?" Gabriel nudged Lian.

"Yeah, I wonder what they were eating." Lian stared back at the red-haired man.

"Sheep, obviously...and a *lot* of them." Gabriel whispered back.

"Alright class," Professor Snodgrass looked over at the elderly man now standing at the doorway, "go ahead and take a look around, and we will meet right back here at noon for lunch."

Gabriel looked around at all the different signs pointing at various rooms. "Well, where should we start?"

"This way I guess." Lian turned towards the sign that read *Cretaceous Period.*

They walked into the large room, and were now surrounded by massive-sized dinosaurs.

"Let me guess...these creatures were like the Tasmanian Tigers of their day?" Lian stared up at a large three-horned Triceratops in front of them.

"Nope, I'm afraid the Triceratops was the sheep." Gabriel turned around to point up at a large Tyrannosaurus Rex. "*That* was the tiger."

Lian looked up and nodded. As Gabriel read the information on the Triceratops and Tyrannosaurus, Lian walked over to a small dinosaur exhibit in the corner. Even though the dinosaur was only half the size of some of the others, there was something special about this six-foot specimen. Lian could not put his finger on it, but maybe it was the way its eyes seemed to face forward, or maybe it was the intelligence he sensed it had. There was something truly different about this dinosaur.

"Interested in that Troodon, huh?" Gabriel joined Lian at the display.

Lian looked down at the sign. *Troodon Formosus.*

"Does it remind you of anything, Gabe?" Lian looked at the way this dinosaur stood on two feet. He studied its hands having two partially opposable thumbs. Its long arms folded back like a bird, and were grasping out in front of it. Something about it seemed so familiar.

"You know...I think it does." Gabriel put his hand on his chin. "It reminds me of...hmmm...oh, I know. *Professor Cordovak.*"

Lian rolled his eyes and shook his head. "I'm being serious."

"So am I." Gabriel thumped his finger into his chest. "She's one ugly lady. It says here that 'Troodon' means 'tooth that wounds' or 'wounding tooth' in Greek, and 'Formosus' means 'beautiful,' which is a little bit of a stretch, wouldn't you say?"

Lian nodded his head, "I'd say...but from a dinosaur's perspective, who knows?"

"It's also thought to be the smartest of all the dinosaurs."

"Really?" Lian turned to start reading the card.

"That's what it says. This guy also had great depth perception, which was pretty rare for any dinosaur."

"Hmmmm...it seems the more we see and read about this creature, the more familiar it becomes."

"It also says here, 'Modern descendants of this dinosaur include Professor Cordovak.'"

Lian groaned in playful disgust. "You don't even have her this year and you are giving her grief. Come on, let's go."

"Okay." Gabriel walked a few steps and stopped. "Hey, you weren't talking about the statues again when you said there was something familiar about this, were you?" Gabriel quickly searched his friend's face for the answer, and then raised his eyebrows in the air. "I hate to break it to you Lian, but everything does not look like those statues."

Lian glanced back at the dinosaur. "Yeah, you're right. But you have to admit that dinosaur has a familiar look about it, and it's pretty different from the others."

"Do you *want* me to say it again?

Chapter Thirteen

The Chamber

Lian entered the locker room and saw Jimmy and Gabriel with their backs facing him. He walked toward them and stopped in front of his locker. The long rectangular lockers were all dark green. He put his hand on the palm recognition pad on the front panel of his locker, and as soon as the scan was completed, it opened. Lian pulled out his green Tri-Asterisk shirt and the gold sports shorts. He quickly got dressed and turned back to Jimmy and Gabriel who were tying their shoes.

"I could really use this class today…it's the one class I'm good at." Jimmy smiled slightly, although the tone of his words seemed more serious than they were in the cafeteria.

Lian noticed he looked really tired the last couple days. His eyes had dark circles under them and his skin appeared pale, his face flushed. Lian determined Jimmy must be staying up late studying, and therefore getting very little sleep.

Gabriel pulled open the heavy door of reinforced steel as they walked together into the huge physical training room. They moved toward the center of the room where most of the students had already gathered.

"I wonder what's in store for us today." Gabriel watched as First Sergeant Gunnar walked quickly but rigidly towards the circle of students.

"Line up, cadets. What are we standing around for? Let's go." His gruff voice echoed throughout the massive room as his hands went to his sides and rested on his hips. Gunnar always referred to the students as his "cadets," stemming from his many years at The McClain Military Academy. He remained very military-looking in every respect. He wore military-issued camouflaged fatigues, his pants bloused into black combat boots buffed to a mirrored finish at the toes, and underneath his beret, his hair was kept very short-almost shaved on the sides. A very nice looking man with a chiseled face and cleft chin, Sergeant Gunnar stood at six feet tall and had a strong and trim V-shaped body. "Let's move it, ladies."

The students rushed into their usual rank and file positions, and Gunnar eyed the columns and rows as he walked slowly around the group. Lian, Jimmy, and Gabriel stood in the same row and remained perfectly still as the sergeant finished his inspection of each column.

"Outstanding. Outstanding, cadets." He moved directly in front of the students, and again put his hands on his hips. "Today we are going to work in the Antigravity Complex in the far section of the room over there. When we speak in terms of gravity, you must remember the whole universe is based on gravity, in addition to attraction. Without gravity pulling us down here to Earth, we would all just float out into space, so luckily gravity is based on the Earth's rotation. Even though we feel like we are stationary, we are actually moving at a speed just shy of one thousand miles per hour as we rotate. Our antigravity room eliminates all of that. Follow me, gentlemen."

Sergeant Gunnar made a military left-face and quickly walked straight for the Antigravity Complex where his assistant, Mr. Owens was standing. It was a huge cylindrical chamber, and the machinery standing beside it powering the chamber emitted a strange noise, unlike any mechanical noise Lian had ever heard.

"Let's go four-by-four." ordered Owens, as the students lined up in front of the doors to the chamber.

"Hey, move over there in the other rows and line up with me so we can all go in together." Gabriel watched as Lian and Jimmy moved to the corresponding rows. "This is going to be so wicked."

Gunnar raised his hands in the air, "Listen up, gentlemen. Mr. Owens will send you in by four groups of four. There are actually four separate chambers inside, and you will have approximately twenty minutes inside with no gravity. Once you enter the preparation area, you will put on the weighted boots–one size fits all, and then grab the weighted belts hanging on the wall. You will strap these on good and tight, like so." He demonstrated the proper weighted belt technique. "Make sure you hook all of the straps securely, even the one between your legs. Now, once you enter the antigravity chamber itself, you will situate yourself near the wall, and we will go through some more instructions on how to maneuver yourself. I will guide and assist you in this entire exercise of experiencing something you have never felt before-total weightlessness."

The three friends looked at each other, all of them smiling with the sheer anticipation of flying through weightless fun.

Sergeant Gunnar continued, "When you are done with the weightlessness part of this exercise, you will maneuver yourself back to retrieve your weighted paraphernalia, and put them on. You will then head to the preparation room where you will once again remove your boots and belts, and then proceed directly to the adjoining decompression room. Any questions?" The sergeant looked over his students, "They're all yours, Mr. Owens." He then turned and disappeared into the preparation area.

Mr. Owens sent three groups of boys in and then turned to Lian, Gabriel, Jimmy, and another student. "Ready, men?"

"Yes sir, Mr. Owens." They entered the closest preparation room, donned the heavy belts and put the weighted boots on over their shoes.

"Man, these are heavy. We aren't floating anywhere with these on." Jimmy slid on his second boot.

Gabriel was ready and standing by the entrance to the antigravity chamber. "Come on, guys. I'm dying to get in there." Lian and Jimmy and the other student lined up behind Gabriel, and the door with its layers of seals attached made a whooshing sound as they opened it.

Immediately upon entering the antigravity chamber, each one of the four felt the hair on their head and their arms rise straight up into the air. Sergeant Gunnar was waiting for them, and directed them to sit on the bench by the wall and attach the seat belt. "Get those belts good and tight, boys, and take off the weighted belts and attach them to the clips next to you on the wall. The boots will be next, gentlemen...try to take them off simultaneously, and be ready to float up," he directed.

Lian, Gabriel, Jimmy, and the other boy did exactly as they were instructed. As soon as they freed themselves from the seat belts, each one of them started to rise slowly.

"Woah." Lian rose up quickly. "This is the strangest feeling I've ever had." He looked back over at Gabriel and Jimmy who were both suspended off the floor, and Gabriel was pretending he was swimming through the air. He noticed the other student was doing pushups on his fingers.

"To maneuver yourselves, just lean in the direction you'd like to go," instructed Gunnar. "You can push off the walls with your arms and legs as well to get some momentum built up."

Compressing his body into a charging position, Lian let it spring out toward one of the walls. It worked like a charm, and he readily learned how to move where he wanted. As he pushed off the wall, he learned he could pick up more speed by doing that, and he thought the added velocity made it easier to guide himself around the room. Gabriel and Jimmy also got used to maneuvering as they both tried different things Sergeant Gunnar suggested.

Lian moved to a remote upper corner of the room and stretched his legs out in front of him. It was the most peaceful feeling. Even his heart felt light in his chest. He looked over and saw Jimmy do a flip in mid-air, and he laughed at Gabriel who was fluttering his arms at his sides like a large overgrown bird. He leaned backward, and felt himself bobbing gently up and down. Closing his eyes and placing his hands behind his neck like he was resting on a hammock, Lian could feel himself totally relaxed now, and thought he could easily drift off to sleep. His body was buzzing slightly as he fell farther into a dreamlike state.

Suddenly, he pictured himself standing in the center of the courtyard at Tri-Asterisk in the middle of the statues. He looked down and saw a giant engraved symbol of an eye centered among the statues on the ground. When he bent down to touch the eye, the ground rattled and opened up, and he was being quickly lowered underground. He saw only darkness and felt only cold. Lian jolted awake as he touched a wall, and saw Gabriel and Jimmy were both looking strangely at him. He smiled and moved toward the opposite wall as Sergeant Gunnar announced it was time to move out and let the next group in. The group followed the exit instructions and headed into the decompression room.

"Some class, huh?" Gabriel sat on a couch in the quiet room. "I feel like a new person."

Lian nodded in agreement as they sat there quietly. When they headed back to the locker room, his thoughts drifted back to the courtyard. He never noticed an eye symbol before. *Just a trance, a dream,* he tried hard to convince himself, *but that feeling of being lowered down in the center of the statues was much too real.*

Gabriel and Jimmy were dressing at their lockers, talking about and reenacting some of their moves inside the chamber. Lian also got dressed as he listened to their stories and smiled at their antics. In reality he was somewhere else. He couldn't figure out why his daydream bothered him so much, and what it actually meant. Why would his thoughts go to the statues, and what did the figures represent? As he thought about the sensation of being lowered into the ground through the eye symbol, he felt a chill run up his spine. He shivered slightly as he thought about the dark and the cold all around him.

"If you had one word to describe it, what would you say about this experience, Lian?" Gabriel looked at him and paused.

"Chilling." Lian looked up slowly as he spoke, and without blinking or displaying any emotion stared into Gabriel's eyes. "No...creepy."

Gabriel gave his friend a weird look as the three of them walked toward the exit.

Chapter Fourteen

The Dance

The car stopped at the gate to Annaka's house. Lian glanced down at the purplish-blue tie and then at the purple flowers lying next to him in the seat. He didn't know how far Annaka would take this Indigo thing, and he was worried about how well the shade of his tie and the flowers would match with her palette of colors. Lian searched his coat pocket and pulled out the wrinkled swatch Annaka had given him, unfolded it and held it up to his tie, eyeing one and then the other trying to decipher any difference in the hue. Even though the tailor assured him the custom-made tie was the right color and matched the swatch exactly, the color still seemed a bit off to Lian. He suddenly noticed the car was not moving, and was waiting for Lian to identify himself through the intercom.

"Oh, sorry…uh, it's Lian Hunter. I'm here to pick up Annaka Dimortra." Lian announced, as he fidgeted uncomfortably in the back seat. *Ugh. Why did I have to say "Annaka Dimortra," like they don't know she is a Dimortra? That sounded so stupid.* He silently scolded himself over and over for his nervousness.

The gate slowly opened. Lian noticed a camera perched on top of the gate wall turning to follow them as they entered. The security at Annaka's house seemed almost as elaborate as the academy's system. He wondered why so many surveillance devices would be needed here.

As the car pulled forward, he noticed the lush landscape was manicured like a botanical garden. The Bel-Air style was much different than the Malibu homes of Gabriel and himself. They seemed a world apart. Tall palm trees lined the driveway, thick grass surrounded by many areas of different exotic flowers were strategically placed throughout the yard, and some sections of rare-looking flowers grew around the perimeter. It was dusk out, but he thought he could make out another set of buildings, perhaps some living quarters in the distance. Annaka's house was set far back from the road, and Lian moved closer to the window to look at the full height of the expansive mansion. Dark stonework lined the entrance way and covered most of the front face of the estate. It seemed almost too dark, extremely uninviting.

The thought suddenly hit him he would be spending the entire evening with Annaka. Lian hadn't spent more than a few minutes with her outside of class, and had never been completely alone with this girl like he would be tonight. He couldn't tell if he felt elated, fearful, or some combination of both. The car stopped in front of the mansion's main entrance, and the door opened.

Here goes nothing. He walked up the wide steps to the front door. He glanced down at the mosaic tiles engraved with a scrolled "D" in front of the tall double doors. He suddenly got a weird thought in these surroundings that he was at the residence of a high government official. He couldn't explain why that thought entered his brain, but it was there nevertheless. The door slowly opened, revealing a tall thin man in a tuxedo. The man had a thin nose pointing upward in a snooty-like manner, heavy droopy eyelids, and he gave Lian a look that seemed almost void of expression. He also noticed the skin between his chin and throat drooped down slightly below his collar and hung in front of his bow tie, reminding Lian of a turkey neck. The man's green eyes moved back and forth over Lian's face, carefully studying every feature.

"Good evening, Mr. Hunter."

"Mr. Dimortra, I'm very pleased..." Lian nervously offered a handshake, but stopped quickly and retracted it when he noticed the man's eyebrows raise and glance down at Lian's hand as if it were a claw.

Their eyes met again, and the man cleared his throat. "Right this way, sir." The man spoke in a deep and heavy British accent.

Lian entered the house as the door shut behind him, his face obviously tinted with an embarrassing red glow at calling the butler Mr. Dimortra. He continued to follow the man through the foyer, his eyes looking down at the heavy beige and white swirled marble floors. The marble was so shiny it looked like glass. He looked up at a giant chandelier, its light springing off the floor like a mirror, most likely making the foyer the brightest room in the home. Two staircases lined both side walls and curved up to meet at the balcony above.

The butler led him to a dark room that appeared to be a study. It had dark red mahogany molding lining all the walls and bookshelves. The ceiling was lined every two feet with large dark oak beams. The butler announced Lian's presence and then exited the room, leaving him standing behind a man sitting in a large dark brown leather chair. Lian heard a click and then saw a cloud of heavy smoke swirling up from Mr. Dimortra's chair to the ceiling. The smell finally hit Lian as billows of cigar smoke continued to fill the room with a dense fog. Lian stood there uncomfortably as a tickle in his throat was getting harder to suppress. He was desperately struggling to hold back a cough as he watched more cigar smoke trailing after Mr. Dimortra, who suddenly stood and walked forward to his desk. Not knowing whether to enter further into the room or just stand there, Lian chose the latter. The fifteen seconds that went by felt like an hour as the man finally spoke.

"Annaka has told me about you." The man said in a deep raspy voice.

"Yes, sir," Lian responded weakly from the smoke.

"Don't just stand there, son. Come sit down, make yourself comfortable." Mr. Dimortra pointed at a plush leather chair directly in front of his desk.

"Yes, sir. Thank you, sir." Lian wished he had more to add to the conversation, but was only drawing a blank at the time.

"You know, I went to the academy with your father, Lian." Mr. Dimortra turned his attention to the fire crackling in the large ornate fireplace. "Julian Hunter…always heard he was a good student, and a very good soccer player, at least from what I can recall." Now Annaka's father moved forward in his seat and stared directly at Lian. "But, that was a long time ago."

Lian gulped, still trying to fight the tickle in his throat. This time he could not respond at all. He was trying to think if he had ever felt this uncomfortable in his life, but no other time was coming to mind. Mr. Dimortra then turned back slowly toward the fire. He was a stocky man, his black hair was slicked back, and he had very penetrating eyes, just like Annaka's. When he talked, the cigar moved up and down with every word, because it never seemed to leave the side of his mouth, held in place at his lips between his three fingers and thumb, with his pinkie finger pointing straight up in the air. Lian wondered if his hand was permanently affixed in that position.

"He's a fine man, your father," Mr. Dimortra continued. "I heard he is doing very well at his new position. Let's just hope the apple does not fall far from the tree."

Lian felt even more uncomfortable now by the harsh tone in Mr. Dimortra's voice, and just sat there as this huge man turned around, making Lian a target of his stare once again. Unsure of how to respond, Lian was relieved when the butler's voice rang through the room and broke the uncomfortable silence.

"Miss Dimortra will see you now, Mr. Hunter."

Lian looked back to Mr. Dimortra, who had turned away from him again and toward the fire as if to dismiss him. Lian's lips parted, but the words to politely exit the room escaped him, so he decided to silently follow the butler back to the foyer after squeaking out a feeble "Thank you."

Annaka stood under the heavy chandelier in the foyer. Her long black hair was all pulled back very tightly on top of her head in a bun shape. Her dress, although it fit her form perfectly, was a much more reserved style than Lian was used to seeing. He'd become so accustomed to seeing her in her tight school uniform that anything else she wore would be a surprise to him, and this dress which covered a lot more of her was a perfect example of that.

When Lian entered the room he noticed Annaka's eyes immediately darted down to his tie-weighing the color to the corsage in his one hand and the flowers in the other. When she glanced back up at him, he was waiting for her eyes to disapprove of the shade of indigo, but she said nothing as she stood there with her eyes penetrating his. She seemed to be waiting for him to say something as she stared at him. As he nervously raised his hand to wipe the sweat from his brow, the purple flowers pushed into his nose and eyes. He coughed as he backed his head up from the incident, and some of the flowers fell to the foyer floor. Lian looked down at the fallen foliage and back up at Annaka. Her mouth stood agape as her eyes pierced his.

"Oh, uh...these are for you." Lian went down on one knee as he scooped up the flowers on the floor and then stood again, his foot sweeping as sly as possible some of the petals still left on the floor behind him. "They grow wild around our house and uh...well..." He paused when he saw Annaka turn to the butler who quickly grabbed them from Lian's hand and walked out of the room. He got the distinct feeling she didn't care for wild flowers, at least the types freshly picked off a floor. He grimaced, he should have bought flowers. Why did he not do that? He started questioning other things about that night as Annaka interrupted his thoughts.

"Shall we go then?" her voice sounding very proper.

Lian realized this was a completely different side of her he'd never seen. He held out his elbow and guided her toward the door. The butler opened the tall front door on the right, stood by as they left, and slowly shut it behind them. Lian stepped to the side as the car door opened so Annaka could enter first. She slid into her seat and once she was in, he walked to the other side and sat next to her in the backseat.

The scent of her perfume filled the car, but even that was a little different than what he remembered her wearing at school. Lian felt strange as they sat side by side-so close, yet he had never felt so distant from her as he did now. It was as if Annaka put up this fortress wall only coming down when she allowed. A visual of a castle drawbridge came into his mind, lowering to allow the peasants in, only to trap them inside the fortress walls. It would have been more comfortable thinking of her as the damsel in distress in the tower, waiting for her Prince Charming to rescue her. Needless to say that wasn't going to happen with someone as strong-willed as Annaka, and he laughed a little to himself at such a silly thought.

Lian swallowed hard and felt he should say something to get a conversation started. "You know I heard this dance is supposed to be..." his words stopped short, as Annaka planted her full lips onto his. Lian saw Annaka had her eyes closed, and then felt his own eyes go from wide open due to the shock of her kiss to fully closed as well. He fell into a dreamlike state. He felt so light, her kiss was so soft, so sweet on his lips he did not want it to end. But it did. He felt Annaka's soft tongue touch his lips as she removed her kiss, a sensation unlike any other he'd ever felt before. Lian sat there motionless with his eyes closed, his lips still pursed, and the skin on his forehead pushed up in a surprised expression.

"Lian," Annaka softly called in a near whisper. "Lian."

He slowly managed to open his eyes to see Annaka with a sly grin on her face. Slowly regaining his composure, Lian grinned, and sat back in the seat, all the while admiring Annaka's beautiful face.

By the time they arrived at the dance hall, he realized most of the drive was spent looking at each other, but no more than a few words of small talk were spoken the entire time, especially after she had kissed him.

The car stopped at the entrance and Annaka's door opened. Lian got out and rushed over to help her. He was relieved to see Gabriel and his date by the front door. He remembered how he had wished earlier he was just hanging out with his friend and not burdened with the thoughts of this date. The entire night made Lian feel so out of place, the *faus pax* with the butler, meeting Annaka's father, dropping the wrong choice of flowers, and the thoughts of an uncomfortable drive to the dance. That all changed with the kiss. He could feel Annaka's eyes on him as she laced her arm into his, and he smiled big as they walked together through the front door where Gabriel and his date disappeared.

The hall was elaborately decorated and classical music from the orchestra at the front filled the room. Lian looked around and realized he recognized many students, although he hadn't yet spoken face-to-face with many of them. All of the students seemed so much older now that they were out of their school uniform and into formal wear. The demeanor of the room was strange, and felt stuffy to Lian, who preferred the ocean breeze on his four-wheeler to this environment. This atmosphere reminded him of some of the formal events he was sometimes forced to attend with his mother and father. Unlike his father, he never found these types of gatherings enjoyable.

Lian straightened up as they entered the main hall. His eyes scanned the room as he searched for Gabriel and his date. He was hoping the two of them could join Gabriel's table where he thought he would feel halfway comfortable. Instead he suddenly felt a tug on his elbow as Annaka led him to another table of her friends near the center of the room. Lian noticed the round table had large silver obelisk-shaped candles in the center. He had just helped Annaka to her seat and sat down himself when the music stopped.

A woman approached the podium. Lian's heart skipped a beat as he realized this speaker was none other than the Academy's Professor Lovitt, her blond hair flowing off her shoulders seemed to have a reddish tint to it tonight. She wore a long red gown fitting her shape perfectly, accompanied by a long black veil loosely tied around her neck draping down the front and back of her dress. Her entire presence was stunning, especially under the spot lights, and her eyes sparkled as she surveyed the room. It appeared to Lian she seemed to fixate those green eyes on him for a few seconds before she spoke, but he couldn't be sure.

"Tri-Asterisk Academy Students and Alumni, welcome. Welcome, each one of you, to the Annual Academy Ball." Her voice was still reverberating through the room as applause and a couple whistles followed her introduction. "As most of you know, I am Professor Lovitt. It is my pleasure to be one of the chaperones for tonight's event." She began to unfold a sheet of manila paper. "Headmaster Gorvant has given me this message to relay to you. 'Welcome students and Alumni of Tri-Asterisk Academy, and thank you for attending the Annual Academy

Ball. I want to remind you that participating at this event is a privilege, and because it is school related, all school rules apply. With that being said, please have a wonderful time.' That is all he had to say." A few moans and groans and quiet catcalls could be heard, taking the place of applause for the headmaster's announcement. "Well, I just want to add that these kinds of events only happen a couple times in one's life, so cherish tonight-cherish these memories. Please have a magnificent and magical evening." Once again applause and whistles rang out, and Professor Lovitt gracefully lifted the bottom of her gown and stepped down from the stage as the orchestra began again. A long line of servers dressed all in white came out in rows carrying large trays with silver covers. They encircled the tables, and in perfect unison placed plates in front of each of the students.

During dinner Lian was lost in Annaka's eyes throughout their rounds of quiet conversation with each other. He noticed she was nearly finished with her plate, but he hadn't taken one bite. He picked up his fork and began pushing his food around on his plate, his elbow planted on the table and the side of his face planted in his palm, keeping his eyes fixated on her. Inside he felt relieved his anticipated nervousness about the night had completely left him, and he was actually enjoying himself. He sat up as one server came around and removed his dinner plate while another quickly set a dessert in front of him. It was a delicious-looking slice of pie, pinkish in color with a graham cracker crust and a strawberry on top. Lian scooped a small bite with his spoon and turned to Annaka. The pie had a light-as-a-feather texture to it, and he saw she was enjoying it as well.

After dessert was finished and the plates were cleared, the orchestra began again. A few songs went by, the pace was then slowed down to a mellow type of waltz. Lian noticed the floor filling up with other classmates.

"Aren't you going to ask me to dance?" she stared straight at him.

Lian quickly glanced at her, held her gaze, and smiled as she tilted her head back.

"Sure." He pulled out her chair and led her to the dance floor. He noticed some of the other students staring at them as they walked by different tables. Lian turned and she pressed her body into his. He loved the sensation of her so close to him. He could feel her breath, and her familiar scent was again filling his soul, feeding it something it had been missing. He looked down at the nape of her neck, open and bare as they moved as one. He closed his eyes. Finding himself lost in the dance as they kept pace with the music, Lian was becoming more and more intoxicated with her as the song hit its crescendo. He felt like he could stay like this forever in her arms, if the music kept playing or not. The music suddenly stopped, but he remained close, and Annaka kept her body pressed into his. Lian was still waltzing slowly with her, but suddenly realized the music had changed, the tempo quickened with an upbeat song, and students were dancing apart all around them. Annaka loosened her grasp as he pulled away, realizing he had just been drawn into her again. Lian wondered if this time he may have shown her too much about her hypnotic effect on him. He grabbed her hand, laced his fingers between hers, and led her back to the table, where he noticed sorbet had been served. A few of her girlfriends were waiting for her, minus their dates.

Lian looked over at Annaka, and she turned her head to face him and smiled. Her hypnotic eyes locked with his, and he felt the familiar pull toward her again, the excitement still there. Lian noticed some of the boyfriends were returning to the table, but then shifted his attention back to Annaka. She lifted her spoon but kept looking at Lian, and he could not pull his eyes away. He watched as the spoon made its way slowly to her mouth, her soft pink lips parting to welcome the bite, but all along staring directly into his eyes. He felt himself totally lost in her beauty as the spoon touched her lips. Suddenly he saw and heard something very much out of place. A snake-like hissing and rattling sound came from Annaka, and it grew louder as a fork-like tongue seemed to dart from her mouth in a quick flickering motion. Its pronged shape shocked Lian, so much so it jolted him. His chair squealed as it shot back from the table and he landed spread-eagled on the floor. Lian quickly shot up alongside his chair, looked at Annaka, and when he blinked next, the loud sound immediately stopped and nothing seemed out of the ordinary. There was no forked tongue, just her beautifully shaped lips. Annaka had turned her head farther, following the noise made from Lian's chair. She then looked up at him with a befuddled stare, and then elegantly raised her napkin to her mouth as she turned fully around to face him.

"Are you okay?" Annaka placed her napkin back on her lap and cocked her head to one side as her left eyebrow shot up, studying Lian's face. She could tell he was embarrassed, but seemed totally unaware of how shocked Lian was about what he thought he had just seen and heard.

He had a thought he might appear naturally embarrassed on the outside, but his head was suddenly spinning. Was he seeing things again? It happened so quickly he was not sure he saw anything. The main lights in the room were dim, and other lights used to create a party-like atmosphere were flashing on and off, so maybe his vision was just thrown off. Was he just growing paranoid? He could feel himself begin to sweat, while the others at the table were looking at him, and in succession one by one started to whisper indistinguishably to each other. He had to get out of there and away from Annaka and her table of friends, at least for a few minutes.

"Excuse me," Lian slowly pushed his chair back farther from the table. "I'll be right back."

He saw Annaka roll her eyes, and could feel her icy stare following him as he turned the corner. His face instantly broke out in a cold sweat and he was feeling dizzy as he made his way into the restroom. Throwing the door wide open, he quickly walked to the sink, loosened his tie, and turned on the cold water, cupping it in his hands and dousing his face. Lian kept repeating the same phrase, "Wake up. Wake up." Even though he knew he was already awake, and the water was not doing much good at changing anything about the evening. He raised his head and massaged his eyes with the coldness. How could he go back out there? How could he face her after what he thought he had just seen? He stared at himself in the mirror, his face appearing more drawn with every look. He suddenly realized two people were watching him staring at himself in the mirror, and quickly recognized them as seniors from the academy.

76

Their relentless stares made him uncomfortable, so he grabbed a towel off the sink and started blotting his face dry. He knew he had to pull himself together and find Gabriel. He ran his hands through his hair, straightened his shirt, and then walked out of the bathroom. He heard the two seniors whispering something as he walked past them and out the door.

Lian entered the main hall and spotted Gabriel in a far corner. He knew he would have to either wait to talk to him later or risk making a scene now. He took a deep breath and then slowly returned to his table where Annaka seemed to be anxiously waiting for him. He sat back down right next to her, but avoided any eye contact with her. He could not make sense of what he saw, but whatever it was, he wanted no part of it. Lian now realized he was actually afraid of his date. He could feel her eyes on him again as he sat there motionless. He felt as long as he didn't look at her, he could resist her magnetic draw. This was as good of a time as ever to find Gabriel. Annaka cocked her head sideways as he approached her ear.

"I'll be right back...sorry," he whispered.

This time Annaka's eyes shot a barrage of angry darts at him as she turned and watched him walk off.

Lian again found Gabriel in the far corner of the room. He seemed to be having a good time. His date sat close to his side, and they were both laughing.

"Hey Lian." Gabriel stood up when he saw Lian standing at their table. "This is Ella."

Lian shook Ella's hand. She was a very pretty girl with soft features and a gentle smile. Her blond hair was loose and fell in soft curls at her neck.

"Nice to meet you, Ella. Gabe, can I talk to you privately?" Lian asked. His breath was becoming shallow.

"Yeah, sure." Gabriel smiled. He whispered something in Ella's ear and kissed her on the cheek as he got up.

Lian led Gabriel outside.

"What's going on? It's Annaka, isn't it?" Gabriel moved his head downward to see Lian's eyes. "I knew she was trouble."

"You have no idea." Lian slapped his palm on his forehead. His eyes kept darting around Gabriel, worried someone would hear him. Seeing the coast was clear, he leaned in towards Gabriel. "I saw something." He stopped talking when a couple students came out the front door and stood nearby. "I can't talk here, it's not safe."

"Then tell me later, Lian. Why don't you at least *try* to enjoy yourself, and forget about everything that's bothering you. This is supposed to be fun, and it could turn out to be a great night for you if you'd let it."

Annaka was still talking to her friends when they reentered the main hall. Gabriel patted Lian on the back as they both headed back to their respective tables. Lian looked straight ahead, wishing he could run out of the dance and not have to face her again. When he got to the table he could tell Annaka and her friends were deep in conversation, but it abruptly stopped when they saw him. Lian couldn't do anything but sit there at the table while her friends stared at him.

"Annaka, would you mind if we left?"

Annaka's face immediately broke out into a wide smile, thinking Lian wanted some more alone time with her like they shared on the way to the dance. She turned her smile toward her friends, who started giggling with a round of "ooohs."

Lian stood up and looked down at each of her friends as they smiled up at him. He cleared his throat, and announced, "I'm sorry, but I'm not feeling too good."

Annaka instantly shot a deadly look at Lian, gave him a quick up-and-down judgmental stare, and then turned back to the table to face her friends, who were all shifting their heads away from the sticky situation that was unfolding. Lian thought she was going to ignore his request and choose to stay with her friends, but she grabbed her purse and turned back around to him.

"I suppose so," she said coldly.

Lian held out his elbow, but she did not accept the courtesy. They walked out the front entrance, Annaka a few steps in front of him. The car was already out front to pick them up.

"How convenient." Annaka got in and quickly turned her head away from Lian.

There was a dark silence this time on the ride home. Lian could tell Annaka was starting to warm back up to him. As they approached her gate and house, she turned to him. Lian kept his gaze straight ahead, pretending not to notice her, even as she moved closer to him. She was silently calling to him, beckoning him to turn and kiss her as the car door opened. He could feel the draw, but he could not bring himself to do it. A part of him wished he could erase what he thought he saw, just so he could go back to the excitement he'd always felt in her presence. Instead all he could think about were flashbacks of something he wasn't even certain happened, but definitely something he didn't understand.

Lian walked around to help Annaka out, but she had already exited the car and was headed toward her door, remaining a couple steps in front of him. As they stood there at the front door, he carefully avoided her eyes by keeping his gaze down toward his feet. He could feel her breath close to his shoulder and slowly moving up to his neck. His will fought off any desire to turn around and meet her stare or her lips. Just as her front door opened, he looked up and Annaka moved forward to take her kiss like she did earlier in the car. Lian moved his head to the side and dodged her advance. She paused, quickly kissed his cheek, and she was gone. Lian could feel a huge weight lift from him as she disappeared into her house. When he returned to the car, he thought of Annaka crossing over the engraved "D" in the mosaic tiles, and silently concluded, *"D" is for "Danger."*

Chapter Fifteen

The Gold Concoction

Lian let out a sigh as he took his seat next to Calek. *Great. Another fun day,* he thought.

"Today we are going to learn about mono-atomic gold," Professor Cordovak announced brashly. "Also known as White Powder Gold, it's a super conductor acquired from sea water, now found most heavily concentrated in areas surrounding the Hawaiian Islands." Cordovak took a few steps and paused in front of a terrarium.

Lian leaned to his right to try to get a better view of what looked like a small rope curled up on a rock.

"Like the asp...a little goes a long way."

"Pshhh." Calek snickered under his breath.

Lian turned his head slightly toward Calek, keeping his eyes down. He didn't dare try to make eye contact with him. Calek reached over and scratched his right hand, and as he did this, Lian noticed another large Band-Aid on his left hand, and more residue on his work station. *His skin is shedding.* Lian was now positive that's what caused all of those flakes last time.

"You'll notice you each have a small vial in front of you." Professor Cordovak looked around the room.

Lian watched as the center of the table moved up. He leaned in closer and looked at what appeared to be water with a yellowish tint. Calek reached out at the same time to grab one of the vials, and Lian noticed the suspicious left hand also had a large patch of scales on top. Calek quickly pulled his vial back as Lian was grabbing his small glass tube.

"Mono-atomic gold has very interesting effects when ingested." Professor Cordovak stared out at the class, and pointed her finger from one side of the room to the other. "Of course this varies from person to person. Sometimes this gold will allow a person's metabolism to process amazing amounts of information in a very short time. It has been said when enough of this substance has been absorbed according to the certain person's height and weight, it may even allow them access to other dimensions. Sometimes this dimensional movement could be accomplished by shapeshifting, a chameleon-like ability to look, act, and talk like another person."

"Shapeshifting?" Lian looked down at his lab partner's scaly left hand again. "That could clear up some things."

"Theoretically speaking of course, it is all in the mind, but it triggers the areas of the brain to accept it as reality. 'How does this happen within our bodies?' we might ask." Cordovak paused, as she looked around the room for a volunteer hand. "In short, this substance activates the brain to open many large areas in each of its lobes we do not actually use anymore, at least not in today's world. It begins aligning its cells, structuring them so they work together by communicating with each other. Any neurons firing out there? Does this sound familiar to *anyone*?" The class was still silent, still afraid to answer any question posed by the professor. "And this may interest some of you...some cases have been reported when some people consumed this powder, this mono-atomic gold concoction...their physical bodies became luminous." Cordovak looked around as most of the lab partners questioned each other on what they just heard. "That's right. You heard me correctly...luminous...glowing." The professor walked over to her terrarium. "Your assignment is to take these vials home with you, and after you've eaten, because you must take this with food, fill the vial to the top with water, shake for at least two minutes, and then consume the gold concoction. As I mentioned, each of you will experience different effects of this substance. Don't worry, it is totally safe to do this, it won't hurt you. I need you to catalog this experience, in full detail. Your paper should include the physiological and the psychological effects this mono-atomic gold has on you. So I will expect a full report from each of you next time we meet." She turned her back to the class and faced the terrarium. "If there are no questions, you may go."

Lian was confused. He held up the glass tube. The class got up to leave as he stood there. He grabbed his bag, placed the vial in one of the front pockets. He walked over to Professor Cordovak, who had now removed the lid from the terrarium.

"Excuse me, Professor."

"Yes, Lian." Cordovak's back still facing him.

Lian grimaced as he watched her pull a small white mouse out of a box on the counter. "What are we supposed to do with the mono-atomic gold again?"

Professor Cordovak turned to face him. "You didn't hear, or you don't believe what you heard?" she turned and eyed him. "Why...you *drink* it, of course, Mr. Hunter."

Lian watched the asp strike the white mouse quickly. The mouse was now on the bottom of the terrarium, motionless.

"Okay...thank you Professor." He saw the snake adjusting its jaw, readying itself to swallow the mouse head first as he turned to walk away.

"Full report, Lian." Cordovak shut the lid as he exited the room.

Chapter Sixteen

Virtual Map

Lian started to walk around the corner when something struck him on the side of the head. He looked down and picked up a piece of paper folded in a circular shape. He turned around and saw three seniors standing in a circle across the hall staring at him. He looked at the words scribbled on the paper: *A-LIAN HUNTER.*

When he glanced back up, the seniors were gone. He grasped the paper in his hand and squeezed it shut, crushing the paper. Some of the students were starting to talk more about him, and from what he heard, most of the comments were portraying him as weird and strange, like some kind of alien. Even so, Lian refused to be intimidated by anyone, including the seniors. He continued down the hallway, stopping in front of a huge screen on the wall. Above the screen were gold letters that read *Tri-Asterisk Academy Virtual Map.* The map image showed his name and his location above a red dot. *Lian Hunter - Hallway Corridor 5.*

Hmmm...kind of a small map they've got here. "How's this thing supposed to help anybody who's lost like me?" Lian wondered out loud. "I don't see the observatory tower anywhere."

"Franz Halstead Observatory Tower, Level 3, Corridor 22," a voice announced. The map zoomed out and rotated, finally stopping on a map image of a large round structure in another building. Lian looked at the dotted red line showing the route from his current location. He held his panoptic watch up to the map and took a snapshot of his route. He looked down at his watch to make sure the entire image of the map was there. When he looked back up at the screen, it had zoomed back in, and another red dot was now approaching him on the screen with the name *Jaron Thomas* above it. Lian turned and almost ran head-on into Jaron, a longtime classmate who had quickly walked up right behind him. Jaron's father was a business associate of Lian's father.

"Oh. Hey Jaron." Lian moved to the side, trying to put some space between them. He'd met Jaron a few times at various business dinner parties, but always felt a bit uncomfortable around him. He had an arrogance about him making it hard for Lian to relate to him. Jaron smoothed his black hair to the side, his mouth in the familiar curled up smile.

"Hey Lian. I haven't seen you around in a while. Thought maybe you fell into a dark hole somewhere."

Lian shifted his weight uncomfortably, suddenly feeling like Jaron may know about his dreams. "No, no...not at all." His intense gaze made Lian feel like Jaron could see right through him. "Well, I've got to get to class."

Jaron put his hand on Lian's shoulder. "Sure, sure. You know, we should hang out sometime."

"Uh...I'll have to get back to you on that."

Jaron turned his head, and saw Gabriel approaching down the hall. He leaned back in toward Lian, "You do that, because it looks like you could use some better company...some better friends, if you know what I mean." As Lian started to walk away, Jaron grabbed his arm. "Remember...our fathers were best friends at the academy. So, why shouldn't we be?"

"I already have a best friend, Jaron." Lian jerked his arm back from Jaron and started walking over to meet Gabriel who stopped at the end of the hall and typing something in his tablet.

"You'll see how important it is...the company you keep." Jaron said loudly as Lian walked off.

Lian was angry that Jaron would speak about Gabriel that way. He was well aware their fathers were business acquaintances, but had no idea they were friends at the academy, and best friends for that matter.

Gabriel looked up from his tablet at Lian, as they both headed down the hallway. "Everything okay?"

"Yeah. Can you believe that jerk said my dad was best friends with his dad? I just don't think that's true. If it happened to be the case, I'd feel like I don't know *anything* about my father. He is so different from me."

"Hey, fathers and sons are not always alike. Gene pools have waves. Just because your father gets along, or at least *got* along with his father, doesn't mean you inherited the same feelings for his son...right? And maybe, just maybe now...his father's a nice guy."

"Yeah. You make a good argument for selective sterilization...and Jaron should have been selected." Lian looked down and checked the directions on his watch. "I've got to go by my locker before class. Thanks for trying to cheer me up with that logic of yours."

"Anytime, pal." Gabriel headed off down the hall towards his class. "Just keep in mind the gene pool is deep, and we are *all* swimming in it."

Chapter Seventeen

The Break-Up

Lian walked down the long corridor, and he noticed a few groups of students looking at him and whispering as he turned his head around at them. He was getting used to the secretiveness of many of the students, but he still didn't want to be the topic of any conversation, no matter what the subject was.

He caught a girl in one of the groups eyeing him, but she quickly darted her stare back toward the group. Lian already felt like he didn't belong at this school, and from the look on everyone's face, he was always going to be someone who was on the outside of every inside joke.

He turned his head away from the gossip as he started down the hall. He abruptly came to a halt when he saw the reason why everyone was talking. Annaka was leaning on the locker right next to his. She had her arms crossed over her chest, her shoulders pressed against the door as she talked to her friends. Lian thought about turning around and walking the other way since she hadn't seen him yet, when she suddenly turned to face him. It was too late. He bit into the side of his lip as he contemplated how to approach her. He didn't want to be drawn into another one of her games. He continued slowly and got to his locker. A weak "Hello" dribbled from his lips as he held his eye up to the recognition screen, and his locker slid open.

"I haven't heard from you, Lian." Annaka's words had a biting air to them as she spoke. "So, why haven't you called?"

Lian nodded his head and grabbed his backpack, attempting to stall for time. He could feel the tension of her eyes still on him. He felt like prey purposely let loose, only to be easily caught again by a predator.

"I...uh...well, I've...uh...I've just been busy." He kept his eyes forward as he spoke to avoid any eye contact. There was a part of him fighting against everything he was thinking and everything he wanted to say, the part wanting nothing more than to be near her. He took a deep breath, trying to maintain control. The thought of her forked tongue suddenly flashed through his head, and he remembered why he wanted to break away. "You know, I was planning to. I really was. I just don't know if I have enough time to spend with you...it's just with soccer and all..."

Annaka moved in close to his ear, "You know, on second thought-don't bother. It is what it is." She pulled away and her voice got louder, "And if it is anything like our date at the dance the other night, I think we should forget about seeing each other at all." she hissed and then turned away, whipping her hair again and walking down the hall with her friends.

Lian did not know whether to be happy or upset he had finally gotten the Annaka situation off his back. In one way he was relieved his relationship with Annaka was over, but in another he felt emptiness, like he had just lost a part of himself.

"Women." He raised his eyebrows and began walking toward the observatory for his next class.

Chapter Eighteen

Written In The Stars

"But the stars that marked our starting fall away.
We must go deeper into greater pain,
for it is not permitted that we stay."
—**Dante Alighieri,** *Inferno*

Lian made his way through the halls, occasionally checking the map on his watch, and finally reaching a passageway leading to his destination, The Franz Halstead Observatory. He looked through the glass ceiling in this part of the entrance hall to the observatory and saw the dome-shaped roof. The panels were open and Lian could see the tip of the massive telescope. The walk was slightly uphill, a constant and slow climb because the observatory was built upon a hill, prominently sitting above the rest of the campus buildings.

Lian knew Franz Halstead was a world renowned scientist who taught at the Academy years ago, before he gained his fame and fortune. He made several donations in the form of grants, and picked up the entire tab for the construction of this new observatory.

He reached the double outer doors to the observatory, and as they opened up he allowed one of the female students to go before him, and then entered himself. It was a massive building, yet the shape and the way the walls curved inward gave him a claustrophobic feeling. The seating was circular, and he found a seat across the room. A few more students walked in, and Lian took out his tablet for notes. He noticed the doors for the telescope closing. Professor Lovitt moved toward the center of the inner circle of the massive room, and began.

"As you are all aware, this is what you would call the "maiden voyage" of the Franz Halstead Observatory. You should be very proud you are now part of this building's history. Today is the very first time this facility is being used for educational purposes, and not only am I the first instructor to teach an astronomy lesson in this highly advanced marvel of science, but *you* are the very first class to experience this phenomenon." The students enthusiastically applauded, some whistled loudly. "With this in mind, I am so honored to present Professor Emeritus Franz Halstead. He is not here, of course. But he has recorded this holographical presentation in honor of this special historical event, the official opening of the Franz Halstead Observatory." The students began to applaud once again as the lights dimmed down, and a glimmer of light started to materialize in the center of the main floor. The light became more focused and in another instant a figure appeared, not quite translucent, not really transparent, but very life-like for a hologram.

"Good morning, ladies and gentlemen. I must admit I am merely assuming it *is* morning right now as you watch this...hahaha. Welcome to the grand opening, the ground-breaking ceremony, if you will, to the Franz Halstead Observatory. I happen to know quite a bit about this new technologically advanced structure, mainly because I happen to be Franz Halstead, as the lovely Professor Lovitt has pointed out to all of you." Halstead's image held its outstretched arm toward where the professor stood, who looked back at the image and affirmatively shook her head, and mouthed "Thank you."

Lian, as well as most of the other students, realized this was just "part of the show," and all planned out ahead of time by the two professors.

Professor Halstead was a short and very thin-looking man with horn-rimmed glasses who sported a bright red bowtie with his brown tweed suit. "After teaching here at Tri-Asterisk Academy for twenty-two years, I became interested in redesigning telescopes, specifically the various lenses to make them more efficient. That industry turned out to be very kind to me. Its success allowed me to pursue another one of my passions, designing observatories. I have studied the structures of a seemingly endless number of various observatories over the years and all over the world. I have designed *this* building by borrowing the best ideas from some of the best. I then created and innovated some other ideas of my own. The end result being what you see before you now. What your eyes will behold in future classes here, as all of the technology I have incorporated inside this observatory unfolds, will simply amaze you. Even this image of me that you see before you right now is one of those advances. Obviously it is a holograph, but a new type using Celutian Particles creating a more life-like appearance of whatever image is projected. Can you imagine the detail of each heavenly body as it appears right in front of you in three-dimensional clarity? Right here behind me is also one of my company's huge telescopes equipped with selective multiple lenses, including the world's most powerful 10-terrabond X magnification. I also included holographical notebooks for each and every seat in the arena, and many more features too numerous to name at this time. Rest assured you will experience all of this technology as the school year progresses."

Halstead looked up and slowly turned three hundred-sixty degrees as he continued. "It has been a pleasure to address all of you today. Have a wonderful school year, and please enjoy this observatory into which I have placed so much of my heart and soul. Remember ladies and gentlemen, I believe in you. So, believe in yourself. Goodbye, and take care." As quickly as Halstead's image appeared, it was gone, and the lights slowly came back on to a low dim.

Professor Lovitt walked down toward the main floor again, but this time stopping on the bottom step. "Such a wonderful presentation from such a wonderful man, wasn't it?" The students once again clapped and cheered. "Yes…even though he cannot hear us, he deserves this applause and so much more." As the applause died down, Lovitt walked to the center of the main floor and touched the control on the belt of her gray skirt.

"Throughout history people have used the stars to foretell future events," Professor Lovitt also began to turn in a full circle as she spoke. The room went black once again and stars encircled around the class. "Many cultures even used an astrolabe, a very ancient astronomical instrument which was used for navigation purposes. Of course, now we have more advanced technology."

Lian stared at the shiny dots forming clusters surrounding them. His eyes quickly glanced down and he noticed all of the students were equally transfixed by the softly blinking lights and the glow given off by the stars. These heavenly bodies gave him a feeling of weightlessness the way they hovered in the air, defying gravity, just as he had in the anti-gravity chamber during physical training class. The images above Lian rotated again, and little balls of light seemed to move right in front of his face. He noticed other students across the room were ducking their heads and swinging their arms at the small lights in front of them.

"Here we have the "Water Bearer," which depicts a man pouring water from a jar." Professor Lovitt pointed at the name under the magnified group of lights forming the constellation. "Aquarius, as we know, is also an astrological and birth sign some of you may fall under, if you were born on or between January 20th to February 19th. I won't bore you with the Aquarius characteristics, but it is the eleventh zodiac sign ruled by the planet Uranus."

Lian noticed the professor's hair looked a darker red color in the light from the above projection. He couldn't help but stare at her profile as she stood next to him. Something else had changed about her physical appearance as well. Her features suddenly seemed to be a little different. She was still a very beautiful lady, but he couldn't tell if her face shape seemed to be a little longer, if her nose seemed to be a little shorter, or what it was exactly. Why did almost everything in his life suddenly seem so different to him? Could it be he was now finally awake and could actually see things for what they truly were? He felt himself jump slightly when her eyes turned toward him. He swallowed and quickly turned away, feeling like she was now watching him. He moved his head to the side as more lights swerved into his line of sight, and he swatted at them as if they were mosquitoes. As Professor Lovitt took a few steps back toward him, the stars rotated to the right. Lian turned his head to look at the lights behind him still dancing and annoying him. He once again took a swing at the lights, but this time his hand came into contact with the back of Lovitt's skirt. The professor slowly turned around to see a surprised Lian, his hand still paused on her dress.

"There are other ways to get my attention, Lian. You can remove your hand now and get on with your question."

Lian quickly pulled his hand back, "Uhhh...no question, Professor. I...I was trying to touch these lights in front of me, and...never mind, it's...it's nothing."

Lovitt leaned over and whispered softly, "Those lights you see are just reflections appearing now and then when some of these celestial images are projected above."

The professor stepped back and continued. Embarrassed, Lian began to look up again and study the constellation above him. He scanned through the different clusters of stars, reading their names. Suddenly his eyes froze. *Orion the Hunter.*

Lian rubbed his eyes, and had to squint to make out the formation. He knew his last name was part of this constellation, but there was something so familiar about the rest of the name. He also couldn't make out the shape of this constellation. All he could see were stars spaced apart as his eyes traced the lines like a connect-the-dot puzzle, but the shapes didn't seem to have any meaning to him. He was so busy with his thoughts he tuned out the class. When Professor Lovitt's voice grew louder, he turned around and realized her finger was pointing in the opposite direction he was facing.

"Ophiuchus, the "Serpent Bearer" is represented by the constellation Serpens. Known as the thirteenth sign of the zodiac, this group of stars depicts a man grasping a large snake-as if in defeat." She smiled as her eyes turned to Lian again. He often felt like she was speaking directly to him. An overpowering vision of Annaka suddenly enveloped his mind. Her beautiful lips, her hypnotic eyes...but then the tongue appeared, prong-shaped, hissing, and flickering through those same lips, and she was suddenly laughing, laughing at him. Lovitt's voice brought him back to the class once more, "Of course, this is all theoretically speaking. Some scholars will debate it is more of a dance between man and serpent." She raised her arms in the air to accent her point. "A joining together." She clasped her fingers, and once again looked at Lian.

Lian let out a deep breath when the lights came back on and the stars disappeared around them. His mind couldn't stop some of the images, but he forced himself to stop thinking about Annaka. He looked at the place where the Orion formation had once appeared, and this new mystery took over his thoughts. He turned toward the door where Professor Lovitt was now standing. All of the students were filing out, and Lian put his tablet in his bag, slung it over his shoulder, and made his way toward the door. He tried to clear his head, realizing he couldn't wrap his brain around all of this at the same time. It all felt like a puzzle, but luckily some of the pieces were starting to fall in place, as strange as they may be.

"Did you enjoy the experience, Lian?" Professor Lovitt smiled at him.

"Yes, Professor, it was very interesting. See you later." He took a few more steps, and turned once again to look at the place where the Orion formation had once appeared. "Orion the Hunter" he repeated to himself. "Maybe one of those missing puzzle pieces is closer than I thought."

Chapter Nineteen

Stonewalled

"Good luck on the game," Jimmy said as Lian passed him in the hall.

"Thanks, pal." Lian walked into the locker room. He pulled his soccer uniform out of his locker and held it in his hands. *Lucky seven,* he thought as he ran his finger over the large green number seven on the back of his white jersey. Something had changed in him because he used to love playing soccer. Recently it had become more of a chore than a sport he enjoyed. His mind flashed back to middle school on the day they won the state trophy. The Tri-Asterisk team felt so different. Although they were supposed to be a team and play as one unit, it seemed as if all the players were all out for themselves. He remembered his middle school soccer coach saying over and over there was no "I in TEAM." His current teammates seemed like they never heard that phrase.

"Almost ready?" Gabriel was already dressed and stretching his arms.

"Yeah." Lian stood up and put his foot on the bench to tie his cleats. "Hey, Gabe, do you know anything about Orion the Hunter?"

"You mean the constellation...*that* Orion the Hunter?"

"Yeah, that's the one."

Gabriel sat back down on the bench facing Lian. "Well, I know a little. It is one of the more popular constellations, and Orion is supposedly one of the gods, the son of Poseidon...the Greek god of the Seas. I remember that...uh...with the way he is facing in the sky he is actually hunting Taurus the bull...yeah, that's it. I also recall Orion's Belt consists of three stars, which is a way to spot him in the sky."

"That is a lot more than I know."

"Why do you ask? What is the interest in that all of a sudden?"

Lian stood up. "I was just in the new observatory for astronomy class, and when Orion was brought up, I had the strangest feeling come over me...I can't explain it. I mean...I know my name is Hunter and everything, but it was more than that. Hard to explain..."

Gabriel put his hand on Lian's shoulder, "I wouldn't worry about it."

"Yeah, you're right. I'm fine. I was just wondering."

"Alright, then I'll see you out there." Gabriel adjusted his jersey and walked out.

Lian finished tying his laces, stretched a couple of times, and walked out to the field.

"Tri-Asterisk Academy welcomes Conquistador Academy from Spain." the voice boomed through the stadium.

He looked across the field at the other team. *Hopefully they have more manners than the British team,* he thought, as he listened to the coach's pre-game instructions then took his position on the field. He glanced behind him and saw Jaron Thomas. He didn't know whether to be more worried now about the other team or Jaron, who seemed to have it out for him ever since their talk by the virtual map.

The buzzer blared and the game started. Close scoring opportunities were happening one after another, with both teams nearly pulling ahead of the other with every possession of the ball. The crowd was boisterous, showing their exuberance over the closely contended match.

"The goalies are getting a work-out." Lian yelled at Gabriel, who shook his head and got back into position. The ball continued to move from one end of the field to the other. Lian looked up at the scoreboard screen floating above the field. No score with only five minutes left of the first half. He wiped some sweat off his forehead. The crowd was getting louder and rowdier as the end of the half approached. The Spanish team's captain fired a terrific headshot glancing off the Tri-Asterisk's goalie's hand and into the net. The trumpeting sound of a goal scored went off just seconds before the halftime buzzer blared. Lian hustled over to Gabriel as he headed toward the locker room.

"Did you see Jaron? You see how far he was from our goal? What's the matter with him?"

"I saw it." Lian kneeled down to double-knot his cleat laces. "Well, he's not our best player, and I think he's got it out for me ever since that one day in the hall."

"You mean the whole 'Our dads were best friends, so we should be best friends too' thing?"

"Yeah, I think that's it."

"Well, don't worry about Thomas, he's harmless."

Coach Adams was definitely not happy in the Tri-Asterisk locker room as he went over some strategies and brought back some old plays. After fifteen minutes of going over new plans for the second half, the teams were back on the field. The buzzer sounded again, and the game resumed.

Lian ran forward toward the other team. He saw Gabriel across the field blocking one of the players and then heading straight for the goal. He ran ahead and saw Gabriel had a straight shot. Turning a little more to the left, he also saw Jaron running forward from a huddled foot fight of players as the ball squirted loose. He dribbled toward the goal, flanked by four of Spain's defensive players. Gabriel had a clear shot to a wide-open goal if Jaron would just kick the ball.

"Kick it, Gabriel's wide open." Lian screamed at Jaron, gritting his teeth as he ran towards the advancing group surrounding the ball.

Jaron looked over at Lian and ran to the right with the ball, ignoring him and moving away from Gabriel. He then dribbled all the way to the other side of the field and lunged forward to kick the ball toward the goal. As his leg went forward, an opposing leg did the same, and the ball was stolen. Jaron went flying hard onto his back as the Conquistadors headed down the field with the interception. Jaron looked over at Lian and smirked as the trumpet went off and the other team scored. Lian looked back at Gabriel who was shaking his head in disbelief at Jaron's actions. They both realized now that Jaron would rather lose the game than see Lian or Gabriel make the winning goal.

Coach Adams called a time-out, and then signaled for Jaron to come over toward the bench.

"What's your problem, Thomas? Did you not see those boys open?"

"Coach, I had a chance to score," Jaron said, pleading his case.

"You had *no* chance to score with four faster boys from the other team around you." scolded the coach. "You thought it was *funny* you didn't pass the ball to teammates who were open?" The coach moved face-to-face and wildly nodded his head as Jaron's upper body jolted back as far as it could. "Yeah, Thomas. I saw that from way over here. *This* is not a *one-man operation* out there, young man. *This* is a *team.* You sit yourself down on that bench and you *think* about that. If I *ever* see that attitude or that kind of *bone*-headed play from you again, you'll be off the team so fast your *head* is going to spin off."

Jaron plopped down on the bench and put a towel over his head. Gabriel and Lian ran back onto the field, they saw the coach still riding Jaron hard as he walked back and forth in front of the bench.

Tri-Asterisk got back one of the goals within the first three minutes, but the Conquistadors from Spain held on, and ended up winning the match two to one. As the end of the game buzzer sounded, Lian and Gabriel walked toward the bench, and saw the coach knock over the water cooler and start back in on Jaron.

"Hard to believe, isn't it?" Gabriel wiped off his forehead.

"Not so hard. I think Jaron will have a hard time making *any* friends acting like that."

Chapter Twenty

Mono-Atomic Gold

Lian looked across his bedroom at his school bag lying on the floor. He walked over, lifted the front flap, and slid the small tube out. He held the tube between his thumb and index finger and brought it up to the light on his desk. He could barely make out some tiny yellow-gold specks settling on the bottom. He shook the tube lightly and bent forward so close he could feel his eyelash brush the side of the tube when he blinked. Some of the gold specks swirled around at the top and slowly descended back toward the bottom.

Lian stood up straight, still holding the tube out in front of him. He still couldn't believe they were expected to drink this, but figured the whole class was doing the experiment, so this had to be safe. As he walked into his bathroom, he pulled the cork from the top of the test tube, and carefully filled it to the top with water. Lian then put the top back on the tube, checked his watch, and started to vigorously shake the vial. At the two-minute mark he studied the gold concoction once again.

"Well, here goes nothing," Lian proclaimed out loud to boost his confidence, as he removed the lid to the tube, threw his head back, and swiftly drank all of the contents. As he put the lid back on the test tube, Professor Cordovak's words about needing a full report flashed through his mind. He pulled out his tablet and set it on the desk as he sat down in his desk chair. "A full report..." he thumped his fingers lightly on the desk as he sat staring at the blank screen. "A report... about what?" He didn't feel anything.

Lian looked at the time, leaned back in his chair, and sat there a few more minutes. He then scooted his chair out from the desk, got up quickly, and walked toward his bed. That movement suddenly made the room whirl in front of him. Dizziness washed over him, and he felt himself falling. Lian's body twisted and he landed hard on his bed, face up and unconsciously blinking his eyes slowly as white lights zapped peripherally at every corner of his vision. A sound like a train approaching was getting louder and louder. The light picked up speed, and he rocked his body back and forth, rubbing his eyes as images he couldn't make out flashed quickly past him. Lian was flying...he felt like he was actually flying. The noise was getting even louder, but his body felt so light, he thought he could simply fly above and out of range of the sound.

All at once the images and the deafening sound stopped. Complete silence. Lian raised his head slowly and sat up, and opened his eyes. He was now sitting on a floor behind a room full of people in chairs with their backs facing him. Disoriented, he stood up and realized he was in a classroom of some sort.

The more he looked, the more it was evident it was a classroom at Tri-Asterisk Academy. Dark blue uniforms. If this *was* Tri-Asterisk, where were the dark green jackets? He looked over at a man who stood lecturing in front of the class, but didn't recognize him as one of the Academy's professors. As he became more aware of his surroundings, he suddenly realized he and the professor were the only two people standing in the room. Everyone else was seated in desks, not chairs. *The others have to be students,* he thought. He quickly angled his body toward the closest desk, and started to sit down, but froze as the professor looked over toward him. Lian prepared himself to be scolded, but the man's eyes continued past him. Lian stared at the professor, whose arms were now crossed over his chest, and wondered if he was going to say anything.

"Something you'd like to share with the rest of the class?" the professor snapped.

Lian could feel his face turning red with embarrassment. "Me? I don't know wha..."

"No, Professor," answered one of the two students who were talking in the back of the room directly behind where Lian was now sitting.

"He doesn't see me? What's going on?" Lian turned to look at the two students behind him, and back up at the professor, then back at the students, and repeated that motion twice more.

"Then I think it is best you pay attention, don't you?"

"Yes, Professor Gorvant. Sorry, sir."

The professor continued.

"Gorvant? *That* is Headmaster Gorvant?" Lian's mind was racing as he tried to make sense of the scene. He closed his eyes and reached back into his memory banks to try and retrieve what Professor Cordovak said about the possible effects of consuming mono-atomic gold. Lian pictured his fingers going through note cards in his brain, like one would do in a library's small file drawer. He stopped and turned his head toward the class, his eyes darting around the room at the uniforms once again. They stopped on the familiar embroidered "A" on the breast pocket on one of them. He knew this was the academy, but he couldn't make sense of the scene unfolding right in front of him. *Time travel...*he exclaimed to himself, *that's what this has to be.*

Lian began feeling a little more comfortable with his surroundings now, a little more at ease with his epiphany. *This is the Academy years ago. But how many years ago,* he wondered. He quickly began to calculate, *Let's see...if that is Headmaster Gorvant...then it must be at least twenty, maybe twenty-five years ago...maybe even more.*

He turned to study each of the students more closely. He was trying to pick up on some of the conversations, seeing if he recognized any names. The Academy was a generational institution, where the current students' fathers and grandfathers attended as well. Lian concluded if he heard a last name he recognized, he may be able to identify the parent or parents of one of his classmates.

He listened intensely for a while, but nothing in the way of names registered as anything familiar. As he looked behind him at the two disruptive students again, his eyes suddenly widened. He recognized the hair, the eyes, and the young face on the one who was whispering to the other...the disruptive one. It was his father, Julian Hunter. He looked at both of them as they started laughing quietly when Professor Gorvant turned around and walked to the other side of the room. Lian tried to figure out who the other student could have been. He had the feeling it may be Jaron's father, but only because of the family resemblance. Lian stood up, and walked back toward the desk next to the one his father occupied and sat down. Turning directly toward his dad, he reached out to grab the back of his father's hand, and was shocked when his hand went right through it, like a ghost.

Suddenly Lian felt the flashing images zapping toward him again. He stood up, bent forward and put his hands out in front of him as lights beamed in every direction. Just as quickly as they began, the lights and images stopped. He looked around. He was now in a dark room. He strained his eyes to try to see anything as he took in the perimeter of the room. As he moved forward, his vision slightly returned, his eyes acclimating to the darkness. He noticed the room was empty except some long garments, possibly red robes hanging on hooks on a wall.

Instantly the flashing lights were zooming past his eyes again, and he felt himself teetering back and forth on his heels. He shook his head rapidly, like a dog would shake off water. Lian was now in what appeared to be a jungle. A howling noise boomed out, and he turned his head quickly to the right. Something flashed past him and was now hidden by the foliage surrounding him. Fear instantly moved through him, but just as quickly disappeared, because he realized this was just in his mind. This was not really happening...he was not really here. Curiosity took over as he headed for the sound. The canopy of the trees became so thick it blocked out much of the sunlight, and the environment got darker with each step. Lian brushed back some large leaves and tried to look around the thick trees. "Where am I now?"

He suddenly picked up a small gurgling noise, and it was getting closer. Lian stretched his neck out as far as it would go to search for the source of the noise. He stayed perfectly still, his eyes moving from side to side, looking toward the sound, when something moved. He stood there motionless as he spied a huge green lizard about half his size. When it ran past him on two legs, he instinctively leaped back, tripped over a branch, and landed on his backside. The lizard vanished as quickly as it had appeared. "What am I doing?" He heard a branch cracking above, and when he looked up, he saw what appeared to be a pterodactyl perched on one of the tree branches high above him.

"Dinosaurs?" Lian questioned.

Once again the flashing lights engulfed him, but this time as he fell backwards, he felt himself move into unconsciousness again. When Lian came to, he immediately moved his hands up over his head, and then cupped his face. He rubbed his eyes once again, and when he opened them he instantly recognized the familiar clock on the ceiling above his bed. He cautiously looked around his bedroom to make sure he was not still dreaming or moving into another dimension.

Surprisingly, he felt refreshed. Lian sat up on the corner of his bed, moved to the tablet on his desk, and immediately started to write his report on the effects of Mono-Atomic gold. The first sentence came easy for him...

"There really *is* no place like home."

Chapter Twenty-one

The 1934 Catacombs

Lian stood staring out his window. It was dark black outside except the reflection of the crescent-shaped moon hanging low in the sky, giving the ocean a luminous green color. He pushed a small circular button next to the sill and the window slid open. A small gust of wind blew in, bringing the smell of salt water to his nose. He closed his eyes and tilted his head back.

There were so many things to which he wished he had the answers. His report for Professor Cordovak was still fresh on his mind and in his tablet. Lian knew he had been to a place in his mind few people, if any, would ever experience. He opened his eyes and stared at the vast openness stretched out before him. A light was now moving slowly over the ocean, he leaned in toward the window and tried to get a better look. The ball of light seemed to stop and was hovering over the water. Suddenly the light disappeared.

Probably just a light from a ship. Lian thought. He shivered a bit and felt the hair on his arms stand up. It was getting chilly out, so he reached over and pushed the button and the window slid closed.

He walked over to his desk and sat down. He looked at the computer screen and the background picture of him posing with his mom and dad. He looked at his mom, her beautiful smile, and the glow emanating from her with her light hair and pale skin. His eyes then moved to his father's face, more chiseled, dark, and defined. Julian's smile was reserved, and his expressions always seemed more serious in every picture Lian ever saw. As he moved to his own image, his eyes stared back at him, and he tried to distinguish his own features from his parents. Who was he? He wondered which parent gave him the more features? His computer suddenly made a beep.

"Message received." a male voice spoke.

Lian looked at a picture of Gabriel next to a small box.

"Open," Lian commanded. A news clip appeared on the screen, a newswoman in a suit was speaking.

"Authorities are searching for another missing girl in the Los Angeles area. Fifteen-year-old Angela Thomas is the second girl within the last two weeks to have disappeared. Angela was wearing a white blouse and a checkered skirt. She is thin and stands five feet, two inches tall, with blonde hair and blue eyes. She was last seen walking in Ferris Park two weeks ago today.

"Kate Farris, also fifteen, is still missing with no word from any searches conducted the last month. Anyone with information on either one of these girls is urged to contact their local police department."

Lian typed his message to Gabriel.

Do they think these are related?

Lian watched after the box on the monitor closed. He took a deep breath when a picture popped open of Angela Thomas. He recognized her face, and had seen her many times passing by him in the hallway at the academy. He continued typing.

Why aren't they saying anything about the academy? They were both from there.

He looked down at Gabriel's message.

It's pretty obvious someone is paying them off to keep these disappearances quiet. There's a lot of big money behind the academy. A lot of old money.

Lian typed out a reply.

I think you're right. The academy is so secretive. They definitely wouldn't want this news of missing students getting out and making the school look bad. Could you imagine the investigations that would take place? I'm researching some things here. See you tomorrow.

Lian hit the Send button, and leaned back in the chair, placing both of his hands behind his head, his eyes now fixated on the ceiling. Thoughts were gathering in his head from all directions. His thoughts transformed to whispers, *Two girls from our school are now missing and not even a mention of the academy. What's going on with this school? The news stations are being paid off? Who else is getting money to keep silent? The big question here is who is paying out all of this hush money?*

Thoughts of Annaka's tongue now flashed through his head. He thought of the slits in the soccer player's eyes. There was some common thread weaving through these two things, something linking them together that he was missing. The news...*that* was it. Lian sat up quickly.

"Search news...downtown Los Angeles," Lian ordered as he thought of the statue in front of the school. "and cross-check with lizards."

A screen popped up:

Los Angeles Times, January 29, 1934
Lizard Peolpe's Catacomb City Hunted

Lian's eyes scanned across the pages of the old ProQuest Historical Newspaper article in the *Los Angeles Times* by Jean Bosquet, and noticed "People's" was misspelled in the title. It was a long article, and contained various subtitles, a map, and pictures throughout. It described the findings of a geophysicist named G. Warren Shufelt. One picture depicted a man with a hat sitting in front of some sort of machine. Lian looked at the name and began reading from the article's subtitle.

Engineer Sinks Shaft Under Fort Moore Hill to Find Maze of Tunnels and Priceless Treasures of Legendary Inhabitants

Busy Los Angeles, although little realizing it in the hustle and bustle of modern existence, stands above a lost city of catacombs and incalculable treasure and imperishable records of a race of humans further advanced intellectually and scientifically than even the highest type of present day peoples, in the belief of G. Warren Shufelt, geophysical mining engineer now engaged in an attempt to wrest from the lost city deep in the earth below Fort Moore Hill the secrets of the Lizard People of legendary fame in the medicine lodges of the American Indian.

So firmly does Shufelt and the little staff of assistants believe that a maze of catacombs and priceless golden tablets are to be found beneath downtown Los Angeles, that the engineer and his aides have already driven a shaft 250 feet into the ground, the mouth of the shaft being on the old Banning property on North Hill street, overlooking Sunset Boulevard, Spring street and North Broadway.

Lian looked at another black and white picture further down. A number of different figures were standing in a row. They looked human, like ordinary people, but their faces and heads were different. Another figure was hovering above them with its arms outstretched. He read on.

Shufelt learned of the legend of the Lizard People after his X-Ray had led him hither and yon, over an area extending from the Public Library on West Fifth Street to the Southwest Museum on Museum Drive, just at the foot of Mt. Washington.

"I knew I was over a pattern of tunnels," the engineer explained yesterday, "and I had mapped out the course of the tunnels, the position of large rooms scattered along the tunnel route, as well as the position of deposits of gold, but I couldn't understand the meaning of it."

Then Shufelt was taken to Little Chief Greenleaf of the medicine lodge of the Hopi Indians in Arizona, whose

English name is L. Macklin. The Indian provided the engineer with a legend which, according to both men, dovetails exactly with what Shufelt says he has found.

Lian recited the remaining words out loud.

"According to the legend imparted to Shufelt by Macklin, the radio X-ray has revealed the location of one of the three lost cities on the Pacific Coast, the local one having been dug by the Lizard People after the 'Great Catastrophe' which occurred approximately five thousand years ago. This legendary catastrophe was in the form of a huge tongue of fire which 'came out of the Southwest destroying all life in its path.'"

Lian looked at the black and white tunnel map. He remembered hearing something about a fire breaking out and destroying the catacombs many years ago, so he concluded there was nothing to explore or examine to check out the validity of the story. *The Lizard People.* The words kept running through his head. Lian sat staring at the screen, and his eyes now had a misty haze over them. It still was not making sense to him. He leaned his head to the right till it let out a gentle pop and then to the left. He closed his eyes for a second and rubbed them. He was starting to fade, feeling very tired. He looked up at the clock...11:39P.M. He pushed himself back from the desk and walked to his bedroom door. He was tired and hungry and he had some hard classes tomorrow. As he walked out his door he heard his mom and dad talking down the hall. It sounded like they were arguing over something. He heard his name mentioned, so he walked slowly towards their bedroom.

"It's got to be done," Julian snapped in an angry voice.

"Julian...he is our son. I agreed to let him attend the Academy because it was your alma mater, but I will not agree with this." His mother fired back, now sounding like she was crying.

"We have no choice. This goes beyond what we want...it goes beyond anything and anyone. This is how it is meant to be."

Lian jumped when he heard a door slam. He quickly darted around the corner and headed down the stairs. He had never heard his mother so upset. He was wide awake now, no longer tired, and his thoughts were flying through his head as he turned the corner to the kitchen. Was he in trouble? Did they know what he saw? He leaned against the counter. He heard more footsteps upstairs. He held his breath to listen, but the footsteps stopped and there was just silence. Now Lian couldn't help but feel things were a lot worse than he imagined

Chapter Twenty-two

The Change

Calek Fulcan stared at his reflection in the mirror. Moving in closer he discovered his left eye was dilated, the pupil so large his entire eye appeared black. As he gently pushed his eyeball with his finger, his pupil flashed into a vertical slit. The sight of this transformation jolted his head back, and his eye immediately reverted back to its original shape. He wondered if this was part of the change he saw in his brothers.

His attention now turned to the sound of Salem arriving home. Although Calek wanted to ask him about these new physical changes, he refrained from doing so, thinking his brother would probably just ignore him anyway. He was very accustomed to being the youngest in a family of four boys, the "runt" as they called him. Calek also realized even though he may be the smallest of the brothers, he was confident he could handle these changes better than a couple of his older siblings. He didn't yell in fear like his oldest brother, who was crouched in a corner of his room, scratching his arms and legs and screaming. Calek was only eight at the time, but he remembered vividly how he quietly opened his brother's bedroom door and peeked in to see what was causing all the commotion.

He also remembered how quiet and withdrawn his other brother, Tarem, had become once the family returned home with him from the hospital and his tendency for weeks to revert into a fetal position. Nobody in the family spoke about the change. It was a forbidden topic in the

Fulcan home.

Calek now looked down at his wrapped hand and pulled off the bandages. A patch of scaly skin hung from his knuckles, and the itching was almost unbearable. He ran his fingernails over the top of it, softly scratching the tender spot, sending flakes of skin floating toward the floor, and exposing some more green underneath. As he scratched harder on his hand, more small bits of dead flesh kept peeling off.

When he tried to scratch an irritating section between his fingers, he was shocked to find he couldn't open them all the way to do so. He looked down at his hand, tried to will them apart, but his fingers would not fully spread from each other. He then tried using his other hand to yank hard at one finger to free it from the other. He screamed in agony as he pulled at his digits and a searing pain shot through his hand. Calek was in total disbelief to see he had ripped a small section of webbed skin between his fingers. He closed his eyes and grasped his hand tightly to alleviate some of the pain. *Webbed fingers,* he asked himself. He cautiously turned his head and opened his eyes to look down and check once more to see if this was just his imagination. The bloody webbing between his fingers answered that question.

Leaning against the sink with his forearms, he ran warm water over his wounded hand. As the bleeding and pain were starting to subside, he noticed the veins in his left forearm were much more visible. He quickly checked his other arm and saw the same prominent veins. He also realized a definite increase had taken place in the overall size of his forearms. He raised his shirt sleeve, and instantly forgot all about the pain as he admired the definition of muscles in his upper arms.

Calek then looked in the mirror at a little patch of raised skin below his neck. He walked into his bedroom and took off his shirt. He was in awe as he viewed the image in his full length mirror, a reflection of a very muscular physique. Calek flexed his arms and began posing in different positions to display his array of newly acquired muscles and sculptured body. It was happening. He was changing. Slowly he looked up and gazed into the mirror, just in time to catch an evil smile creeping up one side of his face.

Chapter Twenty-three

V.E.R.S.E.

"Has anyone ever heard of the Sumerians?" began Professor Snodgrass.

Gabriel raised his hand.

"Gabriel? You've heard of them?"

"Yes, Professor. I think they were here around the same time as the Babylonians."

"Right you are, my lad." Professor Snodgrass rolled down one of the Old World maps mounted on the wall. "Sumerians were one of the earliest civilizations on record. Many of the developments and technological advancements attributed to the Egyptians and other civilizations were actually derived directly from the Sumerians."

The professor shuffled some papers around on his desk for a few seconds. "Now where did I put..." He paused for a moment. "Oh, well." He turned back toward the map using a wooden ruler as a pointer.

"At the time, Sumer was known as Mesopotamia, now known as Iraq. Yes, uh...right about here on this particular map."

Snodgrass put the ruler back on his desk. "Does everyone have their bearings now? Do you understand where we are on the globe?" He looked around the class for any questions. "Alright then, let's go to our Virtual Electronic Reality Simulating Energizer, or V.E.R.S.E., as we call it."

The professor moved to his computer, a few screens floated right in front of him. He moved the images around with his hand, found the tab on one of the screens, and clicked on it in mid-air to engage the program. The class was now in a virtual realistic area of Sumer.

Lian turned to his right, where the bottom block of a pyramid was now within an arm's reach of his desk.

"We are in the outskirts of the city, and as you can see, by one of the Sumerian pyramids. And yes, I know what some of you are thinking...they had pyramids like the Egyptians, and in fact, were the first civilization to have them. They were arguably their most visual and impressive development."

"Professor, how did they construct these pyramids this early in history?" Gabriel asked.

"We will get to that in just a moment. I *will* tell you they were built mostly for religious purposes. Their high priest, called the "Ensi," was thought of as a demi-god. He would live in the pyramids, and climb to the top during ceremonies using ramps and stairs called "ziggurats." I think you will find this impressive. Some of these pyramids would house as many as fifty thousand rooms."

Lian, Gabriel, and the other students were now out of their seats exploring the details of the nearest pyramid. Lian could feel the heat bearing down upon him as he watched some students taking pictures with their panoptic watches. He ran his hand over some grooved etchings of triangles and lines. The professor was now standing right next to him.

"Class, take a good look at the drawings on the side of this structure. These are called "cuneiform," a writing system developed by the Sumerians, using symbols and pictures. Let me remind you again this was long before the Egyptian hieroglyphics."

The professor walked around discussing other Sumerian advancements, such as the development of agriculture and bronze, and inventions including the twenty-four-hour clock and the wheel.

"Think about it." The professor put his index finger to the side of his head. "All of these inventions, all of these developments, all of these futuristic things came from the Sumerians. And all of these happened in a very, very short time. There are many scholars who think they couldn't have done it without help from some outside source, a source far more advanced than our own."

Snodgrass walked up a few steps and turned. "I want you to ponder these ideas as you explore more of these pyramids. Feel free to climb the steps, but just be careful."

Lian and Gabriel passed the professor, and continued to make their way toward the top of the pyramid.

"I'm pretty sure these were built by auditive levitation, just like the Egyptians. What do you think?" Gabriel turned to Lian and climbed backwards for a few steps.

Lian nodded, a bit out of breath. "I agree. I mean, how else could they have done it?"

They kept climbing, finally reaching the highest of the pyramid's plateaus. They walked over to the edge and sat down, taking in the view from below as they caught their breath. The view itself was breathtaking, and they looked out at the structures of a city in the distance engulfed by the desert. Then Lian suddenly froze as he felt something crawling on his shoulder. He was afraid to look, but knew he had to, and knew he should move slowly to do so. Whatever it was, he just hoped it was not poisonous. Lian cautiously turned his head towards his shoulder, imagining the worst. A large black scarab was now moving down his upper arm. Lian immediately jumped up with a loud gasp, startling Gabriel, and quickly brushed the scarab off his jacket.

"What the heck?" Gabriel looked at the bug. "It's just a *virtual* beetle, Lian. What are you afraid of?" Gabriel chuckled and went right back to taking in the scenery.

As Lian watched the bug crawl away, his eyes glanced up and caught a familiar image on one of the center blocks. He got up and moved toward the structure behind him for a closer look. A depression in the stone revealed a figure with an eagle's head and the body of a human, like one of the academy's statues.

Facing forward and looking down the long steps at other students, Gabriel pointed behind him with his thumb. "Right back there is where the Ensi would have..." Turning to his left, he realized Lian was no longer beside him, but now standing at the exact spot he was describing.

"Do these impressions remind you of anything, Gabe?"

Gabriel stood up and walked up the few steps to join him. "Hmmmmm..."

"They're the same figures as the statues in the front courtyard. You know the ones...the ones in the circle."

"Oh yeah, you're right."

Lian ran his hand over the eagle-headed figure engraved in the wall. The head and fully extended wings were carved in such detail it made the depression seem almost life-like. He kept his hand on the wall as he walked up the last steps of the structure.

"Here's the second figure." He looked down at Gabriel, who was still studying the first one. Gabriel walked up the stairs and was now standing next to him. "This is the human one, Gabe." Lian stared at the long beard and the outstretched hand.

"They had some amazing sculptors back then. It seems like you could pull a hair right out of this guy's beard."

"I know." Lian took a few more steps around the structure, his hand never leaving the surface as he searched for more markings. "But where is the third?" Lian continued to follow the wall around a corner when he suddenly stopped.

"You're not going in there, are you?" Gabriel peered around Lian's shoulder and saw an opening.

"Why not?" Lian stepped through the entrance and turned back to Gabriel, "It's only virtual, remember?"

"Yeah...well, alright." Gabriel followed his friend into the mysterious structure.

Lian looked around as he stepped cautiously. It was pitch black except a faint glow ahead. He kept walking toward the light until they came to another opening. He motioned for Gabriel as he started walking into the next room.

"I just want to remind you about the fifty thousand..."

"Shhhhhh." Lian squatted down. He looked at Gabriel and mouthed the word "Look," as he pointed ahead. A large figure was standing and looking out one of the openings to outside, its back facing the boys.

"It's the Ensi," Gabriel whispered back to Lian.

Lian noticed a large chair at the top of some steps, when suddenly, the figure turned toward them. Lian let out a small gasp, but quickly covered his mouth with his hand to stifle it. It was the third figure, with green scaly skin and the mouth twisted up into a mock smile. But this was no statue. This was alive. Its large eyes shot over at them as it raised its hand and pointed directly at them.

"Run!" Lian yelled, as the two scampered toward the door.

"This way." Gabriel was looking down and running into the corridor, tracing his way back toward the first opening. When Lian looked up, he saw Gabriel run right into the clutches of two human guards, each one holding a different arm. These guards were huge specimens, shirtless with a long loincloth around their waists and ceremonial-looking headdresses. Wrapped around each of their bulging biceps were spiral bands of gold. Gabriel was struggling, trying to get his arms free, and straining to turn around and see Lian. Lian looked around for something he could use to strike the guards so they would release Gabriel, but the darkness kept any weapon like that hidden from him.

Just then Snodgrass's voice boomed through the air, "Class, we are going to return now." Suddenly Lian was back in his seat as the classroom reappeared instantaneously. He turned and let out a sigh of relief as he saw Gabriel sitting next to him, but visibly shaken. Lian looked down and noticed his own hands were trembling as well.

Professor Snodgrass was gathering the papers from his briefcase. "I hope each of you obtained a lot of information from this hands-on experience. I always find being there, even if it is only virtually being there like we've just done, brings the learning to a whole new level."

Lian and Gabriel looked at each other, both still stunned by what they'd just witnessed.

Snodgrass folded more of his notes and put them into a binder. He put both hands on his desk, leaned forward, and then proceeded, "I want you to finish up the small section on the Sumerians on page twenty-nine in your tablet. Most importantly, I'd like you to put some real thought into my previous question. How did all of these advancements come into existence in such a small frame of time? I want each of you to send me a short report on this topic by the end of the week."

The professor snapped his binder, grabbed his briefcase, and tucked it under his left arm. "If there are no questions on the assignment, you can go when the bell..." The sound of the period bell ringing interrupted Snodgrass in mid-sentence. "Well, I guess you can go now."

As Snodgrass and the other students filed out, Lian and Gabriel tried to gain their composure. They turned sideways in their desks to face each other.

"What just happened? Can you believe that? I thought I was a goner." Gabriel was still wiping sweat from his forehead.

"Believe me, I did too. Those guards were *huge*."

"And strong." Gabriel started reenacting that scene with the guards, moving back and forth with his arms stiffly held out at his sides. "I couldn't budge, not even an inch."

Lian stared straight through Gabriel, trying to understand everything he saw.

"By the way, did you see those golden asps they had around their upper arms?"

"Yeah, I saw them."

They both sat there silently for a minute.

"So, the Ensi, the demi-god they worshipped was a...

"Reptile." Lian bit his lip slightly. "I can tell you this...that Ensi thing didn't seem like any kind of virtual reality to me."

"I know. And those guards were more like a *real* reality."

"I didn't think anything in the virtual world could hurt you, like that scarab." Lian put his head down, rubbed his forehead, and thought for a few seconds. "It seems like every time I turn around, every new situation I get myself into here lately, I have more and more things fall in my lap, things I cannot explain. My mind is overflowing with mysteries."

"You've had a lot of things happen to you, and I know you have a lot on your mind."

Lian brought his head back up, "We need to find out what that was all about up there," as he pointed where the top of the pyramid had stood. "I think I know where we can get some answers."

Chapter Twenty-four

The Time Traveler

Gabriel followed Lian as he walked out into the hallway and headed straight toward the front of the building. It was their lunch hour, but the cafeteria was one hundred-eighty degrees behind them as they continued their trek. When they started down the hall of the entrance way with all of the busts of former headmasters, Lian stopped.

"Don't turn around and don't look up. When we reach the doors, just walk and act normal, like we have something to do outside."

They walked at a medium pace, trying not to draw even the slightest bit of attention to themselves. It seemed like it took a long time just to reach the front doors. The doors slid open, and Lian and Gabriel strolled out nonchalantly, moving toward the circle of statues in the courtyard. Lian looked up at the massive sculptures in front of him, as Gabriel nervously took turns looking left then right, checking to see if anyone was watching them.

"Yep, these are definitely the same figures." Lian walked back over to Gabriel. "But why are they here?" Lian looked up at the face of the reptile statue. His mind flashed back to the way the Ensi's large eyes stared at them.

They both began moving around the circle, taking in all of the features of each one. They stopped in front of the eagle-headed figure.

"What about this one?" Lian looked up at the large beak. "You don't think they have one of these things in there too, do you?

118

"I don't think so." Gabriel pointed at each feature. "See the human hands? And this is probably just a mask. I mean, did you see their headdresses? They were pretty elaborate."

"Well, I hope you're right." Continuing around the circle, Lian looked up at the bearded figure towering in front of him. "But, that still leaves this one."

"Well, that's easy."

They looked at each other and said simultaneously, "It's one of us." They quickly looked down at their watches.

Lian furrowed his brow as he pointed at the watch on the figure. "Someone traveled virtually back in time."

"Yep. The Sumerians who witnessed this thought he was a god."

"All of that still doesn't explain why they are here." Lian walked into the center of the figures. "Look here…there's some writing on the back of this one." He studied the lines and triangular shapes. "It's Sumerian, too." He held up his watch and took a picture of the marks on the back of the reptile figure.

"Lian," Gabriel waved him over, "check this out."

Lian moved next to Gabriel to get a closer look. "Lazarus Talon Hunter" was etched into the bronze with seven other names.

"Do you know who this is?" Gabriel inquired.

"No. No, I don't. At least I've never heard that name mentioned before."

"Well, that's strange."

"It's a mystery."

"It's a *strange mystery*." Gabriel imitated an eerie voice while raising his hands hauntingly.

Lian shot him a quick glance, grinned, and continued, "It *is*, isn't it? And we need to solve it."

"Hey. Maybe Snodgrass can help us."

"Get out of my head, Gabe."

Walking back through the main doors, Lian and Gabriel headed straight toward Snodgrass's room. The hallways were still empty. When they got to his room, the door was open, so they took a few steps inside the room and looked around. The professor was nowhere to be seen.

"Professor Snodgrass?"

Chapter Twenty-five

The Map

Snodgrass's room was spacious, but not modern in any sense of the word. It could be called a throwback to the classic antiquated classroom. The only thing lacking to complete that look was a chalkboard. Gabriel headed to the back of the classroom to look at some of the artifacts on the shelves, while Lian moved across the room to investigate an item he hadn't seen before. He assumed the glass jar on the shelf must be yet another new addition to Snodgrass's acquisitions. He kneeled down to get a closer look. The jar held a creature with a pinkish hue that seemed to be floating weightlessly in a clear liquid. It reminded him of a human embryo that still had a tail, but its slit-like nostrils and scaly skin made it look more like a lizard. It was turned in such a way Lian could only see one of its round black eyes that seemed to be staring out at him with a blank gaze.

"Picked that one up in a cave just south of Machu Picchu." The professor's voice startled Lian who quickly stood up.

"Oh. Hi Professor. Very interesting specimen, sir." Lian returned his eyes to the jar.

"Did you need something, Lian?"

Lian started shaking his head "no," but quickly added, "Uh...yeah. Actually I do, sir. Do you know where I can find information about former students of the academy?"

"Former students?" Snodgrass eyed him curiously, and then

massaged his chin with his index finger and thumb.

"It's for research," Lian glanced over at Gabriel who was now walking between rows of desks towards them, "on my own family."

"Oh, I see. Well, there is the Hall of Records. They have information about...well, almost everything."

"The Hall of Records?" Lian repeated.

"Where is this Hall of Records?" Gabriel joined them, but was immediately distracted by the embryo-creature in the glass jar.

"It's one of the older buildings located downtown. It is part of what used to be the academy's campus. I have a map somewhere here in the classroom. Let me see." Snodgrass moved to the other side of the room where boxes of rolled–up maps were stored. The professor moved from box to box muttering something to himself as he touched the top of different maps. "Here we are." He handed a small rolled up map to Lian. "Maps of the academy are hard to come by these days. The department heads tried to collect all of them some years ago, but I kept as many as I could without raising any suspicion about myself doing so."

"Why would they do that?" inquired Gabriel. "What difference would it make if someone has an old academy map?"

"I questioned it myself, and had originally thought they merely wanted different perspectives for blueprints to expand the campus, maybe to build some more buildings. But, that explanation didn't take long to stop making sense to me when no construction took place. I soon discovered..." the professor paused, his eyes moving back and forth between Lian and Gabriel. He then slowly held his right hand out in front of him, with his index finger pointing straight up in the air. His hand then tilted toward them, and with his finger pointing at each of them on every other syllable, he continued, "There are things about this academy that are best left as secrets." Snodgrass then pointed at the map in Lian's hand, and warned, "Remember that, and be careful about who you allow to see this map."

"It'll only be us, Professor. I swear," Lian promised.

"Good. Just return it whenever you are done with it. No hurry."

"Yes sir."

"Anything else I can do for you boys?"

"No, that was all we needed, sir." Lian hoisted his bag over his shoulder. "Thank you Professor."

"Well, be careful." Professor Snodgrass smiled slightly.

As they were walking out, Lian turned and saw the professor still watching them as they left. He nodded once at Lian as the boys exited the room.

Lian looked at Gabriel as the bell rang. "Hang onto this until tonight, okay? I don't want to take a chance on it getting ruined during lab."

"All right. How 'bout we check it out after dinner tonight?" Gabriel took the map and rolled it tighter in his hands.

"Exactly what I was thinking. I'll get the car, and tell Mom we need to do some research. That *is* the truth, I just won't mention where that research will be taking place."

"I'll say the same thing. Hopefully it won't be too difficult to find this place."

"All right then, see you after school."

"Sounds good."

Gabriel smiled and winked at Lian, and then headed off to class with the map in hand. Lian hustled off in the other direction toward his science class. As he made his way through the crowded halls, he wondered what new developments Calek would have in store for him since the last lab. Had he lost more hair? Would there be another chance to see his skin change or flake, or would there be more bandages to hide such things? Curiosity always burned like a powerful fire within Lian, and Calek was certainly one who often fanned those flames.

Chapter Twenty-six

Council Meeting

"We must make sure our activities are kept as secretive as possible, especially within the surrounding communities. I don't mind telling you our recent acquisitions of subjects for our sacrifices are starting to concern me. I believe it may be too much too soon in such a short period of time."

"It is definitely not like the old days, Mayor Harding." Councilman Arthur uncrossed his arms and put both of them on the long gray granite table. "From the local LEO's to the FBI, they've all increased their numbers and their efforts to put a stop to these abductions, mostly due to the outcries of citizens in these same neighborhoods. Obviously, they are worried *their* children could be the next victim of these crimes."

"What makes these matters much worse is the abductees are all female, at least the ones in which we have been involved. You have to remember from the viewpoint of the citizenry, females *should* have more protection…the fairer sex, daddy's little girl, and all of that." Mayor Harding took another sip of coffee. "I also believe we may have to cut back on utilizing the Tri-Asterisk Academy for our subjects, at least for a while. The last three girls were attending that institution, and we may have aroused too much suspicion regarding that venue."

Other executive council members began mumbling to each other, looking around the conference table with that statement, and many were shaking their heads affirmatively.

Tobias Marx raised his index finger in the air, "In all fairness to the academy, we do have a number of high schools to choose from. Although some of the Tri-Asterisk seniors have proven to be quite helpful in successfully capturing these girls, and doing it without any trace of evidence left at any of the crime scenes. They are an integral part of the success of these last incidences."

"I agree wholeheartedly, Tobias. Even better news, the number of these seniors we can utilize to our advantage is growing quite rapidly." Harding took off his glasses as he sat back in his plush chair at the end of the conference table. "I think the person to best comment on the seniors and our advancements at the academy is the headmaster himself." The mayor extended his arm and open hand toward Gorvant, who was sitting two seats to the left of the mayor. "Avontis, would you care to take over and speak on this subject?"

Headmaster Gorvant sat up and began. "Certainly, Mayor Harding. Well, I am, of course, very proud of all students who attend Tri-Asterisk Academy. But our senior classes continue to be exceptional. Year after year they have gotten larger and better, in my opinion. I am more than elated to volunteer the services of our seniors, to let them contribute, let them help our movement in any way they can."

"Very generous of you, Avontis. The seniors presently play, and will continue to play a very important role for us. I think it would be a wise move at this time to feed a story to our friend at the paper...one emphasizing the number of abductions that actually happened at the other high schools in surrounding communities. This will alleviate some pressure and take the attention off the academy. Are you still regularly in touch with our friend at the paper? The editor of *The Los Angeles Sun* is your close friend, isn't he?"

The headmaster surveyed the table as he spoke, "Yes. In fact, we just had dinner together the night before last."

"That is a good idea with the paper. And gentlemen, while we are on spreading our influence as far as we possibly can, I need to inform all of you Congressman Watts will be here at next month's meeting. He wants to give us updates on how our government infiltration is proceeding at both the state and federal levels."

Milos Arthur put his pen down and looked up from his notes on the conference table. "I cannot begin to tell you about the importance of this meeting with the Congressman. I guarantee it will be quite the eye-opener."

"Thanks, Milos. We all know how vital this infiltration of our various governments is." The mayor slowly eyed each committee member from left to right. "Our future depends on it."

Chapter Twenty-seven

The Headmaster

"Everyone is excused..." Professor Cordovak announced as she clicked the preparation button, "...except Lian Hunter."

Lian stood up next to his table, frozen. Looking at Calek's empty stool, he wondered why his lab partner wasn't in class today, and if that absence was the reason the professor wanted to see him. He watched the center of the lab stations simultaneously all move down as the stools and tables rotated, folded up, and disappeared into the floor as well. The floor itself had expanded and covered up the open areas so perfectly, one could never tell full lab stations were beneath them. The other students had already left the room as Professor Cordovak turned to face him.

"Headmaster Gorvant would like a word with you in his office." she looked at him, her eyes unflinching.

"Headmaster Gorvant?" Lian repeated. As his eyes surveyed the floor his mind rapidly searched for reasons why the headmaster would want a face-to-face meeting with him. He had never met the headmaster, and it made him nervous just thinking about doing so. Had he done something wrong? He looked up to ask Professor Cordovak if she had any idea why Gorvant would want to see him, but she had already walked away. Lian grabbed his bag tightly in his fist, turned and left the room. He was halfway down the hall when he suddenly realized he had no idea where the headmaster's office was. He moved down the hall to one of the virtual maps. His name appeared instantly on the map. *Lian Hunter-*

Hallway Corridor 8.

"Headmaster Gorvant's office," Lian said as he looked up at the red dot above his name.

"Headmaster Gorvant's Office, Level 1, Corridor 2, Tower 1, floor 3," the map answered and zoomed out, revealing the red dotted line route to the headmaster's office. Lian held up his watch, took a picture of the path, and then checked the image.

He started walking toward his destination. As he looked at the flashing green dot on his watch, he realized he'd traveled past that area many times. Gorvant's office was located near the front of the school, right off the entrance hall displaying previous headmasters' portraits and busts. He picked up his pace and closed in on Corridor 2 where Gorvant's holographic bust stood. Lian slowed down to walk around it, and he studied the headmaster's eyes as they seemed to watch him, following every step. Lian moved farther down the hallway, he had never been in this particular corridor of the school. He stopped when he came to a large metal door. Above the door and pointing directly down at him was a monitor screen suddenly flashing on and displaying his face and name.

"Access Granted," a computerized voice of a woman spoke as the large metal door slid open. He stepped inside, the doors shut behind him, and the elevator slowly started upwards. Lian nervously scanned the interior, thinking it was extremely plush for an elevator hardly ever used. He looked up and watched the digital dial light up with the floor numbers, and noticed the two additional letters "B" and "L" listed to the left of the first floor. Barely feeling the upward movement of the elevator, Lian's attention shifted to the hundred thoughts racing through his head, still trying to figure out why Gorvant would want to see him.

"Third floor, Headmaster Gorvant's office," the voice rang out, as the door opened into a large open area. The German opera, *Der Ring des Nibelungen*, filtered through the room, and the heavy classical music set the tone of the atmosphere. Lian looked at the elaborate seating area spread out in front of him with expensive furniture, décor accents, and original masterpiece paintings. He figured the headmaster must also hold important meetings with dignitaries here in this impressive environment.

He was strolling past a foursome of galuchat leather chairs when an attractive woman came walking up to him. Her striking blonde hair was pulled up on top of her head, and she wore a nicely fitted suit jacket and skirt. Lian opened his mouth to introduce himself when she nodded her head toward him and cut him off before he could make a sound.

"The Headmaster will see you now, Mr. Hunter," speaking softly but clearly, as she then turned and walked toward a set of double agarwood doors.

"Thank you," replied Lian as he followed his escort.

The double doors opened outwardly with perfect timing as they approached the threshold. Lian looked straight ahead at Headmaster Gorvant who was sitting in a tall chair behind a long marble desk, looking at him. Lian stayed with the assistant a few feet into the office, where she stopped and announced, "Lian Hunter, sir," and then abruptly exited, the doors closing behind her.

"Thank you, Darby. Have a seat, Lian." Gorvant spoke in a very deep voice.

Lian stepped forward and sat on the edge of one of the chairs directly in front of the desk. His head turned as his eyes were immediately drawn to the wall on his left, which was completely covered with monitors. Lian had never seen so many in one spot. He closely studied one displaying an academy hallway, and watched as a couple of students walked by, the screen zooming in on them. Other screens showed various classrooms, Professor Cordovak's being one of them.

Lian felt his heart skip a beat when he saw the front courtyard by the statues displayed on a monitor to the far right. Did Headmaster Gorvant see him out there with Gabriel that one afternoon? Was he in trouble because of this? He suddenly wondered if Gorvant was listening and heard everything they said that day as well.

"Yes, quite amazing, isn't it?" Headmaster Gorvant asked, as Lian turned quickly back to face him. "Busy little bees they are." Gorvant grinned slightly at Lian and looked over at the screens. He then started swirling his thick index finger as he pointed, "It's very interesting to watch the colony as they swarm around, going about their daily business…all with their own little jobs to do."

Lian shifted uncomfortably in his seat. He looked at Gorvant's eyes-so deep set and dark, like small black holes. He thought back and remembered the headmaster's eyes had not changed at all when Lian saw him as an instructor during his mono-atomic gold time-traveling adventure.

"Funny little thing about bees. Did you know it's really the female bees that do all the work?" Gorvant cocked his head slightly to the side as he looked at Lian, who at this point had a confused look on his face. "Oh, yes...the male drones have some uses-without them, there would be no more little bees. After all, some of the chosen ones mate with the queen. The others, I'm afraid, are deemed useless, and forced from the hive. They're left to starve and die."

Lian sat there quietly, not moving a muscle, and unsure of what to say. He watched as Gorvant sat slowly back in his chair, placing both of his arms out on the armrest.

"Lian, you are probably wondering why I called you up here, aren't you?" Gorvant raised his jaw slightly as he continued. "I generally summon every new student, just to see how they are adjusting to the academy."

Lian could feel a wave of relief splash over him as he sat back and relaxed his body a little lower in the chair.

"So, Lian...how are *you* adjusting?" A slight shadow cast across Gorvant's face as he leaned forward.

Lian swallowed hard and squeaked, "Good, Sir. I mean, Headmaster Sir."

"That's fine, just fine." Gorvant laced his fingers over his midsection. "You know, Lian, your father and I go way back. A fine man, your father, a really fine man...and *very* bright." The headmaster raised his head slightly and briefly stared over Lian's head as he spoke. "Julian was an excellent student. I had the pleasure of teaching him one year. As you know, he was also a very talented athlete. And the way he could handle the pressure on the field, well...not many like him." Lian's thoughts zoomed to his blackout during the opening game, and how it must have looked from the sky box.

Gorvant leaned in slightly closer and brought his voice down to a semi-whisper. "Like your father, I'm going to give you some advice." He brought his finger up and pointed at Lian. "Stick with the colony, Lian, and you'll do fine." He leaned back as he folded his hands over his stomach again, paused a few seconds, and then motioned his head toward the door.

"Thank you Headmaster." Lian turned to get up, and as he was exiting the office, he noticed Snodgrass's room on one of the screens. *If the headmaster spotted Gabriel and me at the statues,* he worried silently as he made his way toward the elevator, *he could've continued watching as we got the map from Professor Snodgrass as well.*

Lian retraced his steps back down to the entrance hallway and out the main doors to head for home. Gorvant's words began echoing in his brain, *Like your father...stick with the colony.*

Chapter Twenty-eight

The Talk

Setting his bag on a table by the front door, Lian was relieved to be in the safety of his home, a place where he didn't have to worry about watching his back. There were so many secrets at the academy, and it became an uneasiness he just couldn't get used to.

He walked toward the kitchen and stopped in his tracks when he heard his father's voice. His father was actually home, and now was his chance to hopefully talk to him. He had so many questions about the academy he wished he had answers to.

Lian walked by the kitchen entrance, and peeked in at his mom pulling a roasting pan out of the oven. "Dinner almost ready, Mom?"

"In about ten minutes, honey. Oh, and your father's home. I know you've been wanting to speak with him."

"I heard him when I walked in. I think I'll go up there now." Lian turned and headed up the stairs toward his father's office. He started to knock on the door when he heard what sounded like his father arguing with someone. He leaned in to the door, pressing his ear against it.

"I told you that I don't know. This is all new information to me as well," Julian said in a firm voice. "Alright, alright...I'll see what I can do."

Lian hadn't thought about the pressure his father had to deal with on a daily basis. He suddenly felt bad for getting angry at his father for always working so hard for their family and therefore not being around. He waited for another minute. He didn't want his father to know he'd been listening. Very quiet about his work and never talking about it, Julian Hunter made a good living for his family, although Lian never knew exactly what his father's occupation was. He only knew his father worked for very powerful people, and he sometimes would have a business acquaintance over for dinner or a meeting. But most of these meetings were usually held elsewhere.

Lian started to knock on the door when it suddenly opened, his father standing in front of him.

"Lian. How long have you been standing here?" Julian's voice sounding strained while running his hand through his dark hair.

"I...I just got home." Lian felt uncomfortable at the way his father was immediately interrogating him. He did not seem to be acting like himself, and had an almost nervous demeanor. "I just wanted to talk to you, Dad...about the academy," Lian fidgeted nervously by the door, wondering if his father was going to invite him in.

"Oh...alright," Julian opened the door wider. "Come in."

Lian looked around his father's office. It had been a long time since he had been inside this room, since no one was allowed to go in there when his father was gone, which was most of the time. The room did not look any different to Lian.

He noticed various notes were scribbled on multiple writing screens in the center of his father's desk, as well as a couple large computer monitors perched on each side. His father turned the writing screens over and set them to the side as he sat down, gesturing to Lian to sit as well. Lian walked over and sat in the chair across from the desk, his eyes catching sight of a bronze sculpture of the Tri-Asterisk Academy symbol on a shelf behind his father. Next to the sculpture impressive-looking certificates lined the shelf, all bearing his father's name. *Julian Gillian Hunter.*

"What can I do for you, son?" Julian moved forward, raising one of his hands up and placing two fingers on his temple with his elbow resting on his chair. "Is everything alright at the academy? Your mother mentioned you seemed worried over something."

"It's uh...just different there, I guess." Lian immediately realized his anxiousness to talk with his dad suddenly transformed into an uneasiness making it difficult to open up to him. When it came to the academy, his father had nothing but the utmost respect for his alma mater, and commented many times to many people on how outstanding the school was.

"Different how?" Julian had a very serious expression on his face.

"Well, when you went there, did you ever..." Lian just could not get the words out, and felt like he would let his father down if he asked the wrong question. "...did you ever play any other sports?"

Julian took a deep breath, "Other sports? No, I was always a soccer player, much like yourself-even at the university." Cocking his head sideways, he squeezed his mouth to one side. "Is that what you wanted to talk to me about? Sports?"

Lian felt on the spot. It was obvious his dad saw through his small talk. "Well, there are also some other things-like Headmaster Gorvant. I mean you never see the guy, but it seems like he is always watching us. You know he's around because you always hear him." He paused, trying to choose his words carefully. "He's almost like a puppet master, hiding behind the curtain."

"That is what a Headmaster is *supposed* to do, Lian." Julian stood up, "Now, as much as I would like to sit here and engage in more small talk with you, I really have a lot of work to get done."

Lian stood up, walked towards the door and opened it. "By the way, Dad...was there ever a Lazarus in our family tree somewhere?"

"Where did you hear that name?"

"I just came across it at school today. It said he was one of the "founders," so would that be a founder of the academy?"

"Yes, he was." His father crossed his arms over his chest. "Now like I said, if you'll excuse me, I have some things I need to do before dinner. What you need to do is to stop worrying about things that don't really concern you."

Lian smiled. Closing the door behind him he thought, *Well, that went well.*

Chapter Twenty-nine

Nibiru

Military Operations: Antarctica
South Pole Telescope (SPT)

The helicopter's blades struggled through the blinding blast of snow as the wind hurled drift after drift of the blizzard sideways at the pilot's windshield.

"Is everything all right up here?" Charles White leaned forward with a half-whisper.

The pilot viewed his instruments again, double-checked his location, and looked for a signal on the ground as the copter was being violently shaken back and forth on its descent.

"Yes, sir. If I can't find the landing lights, I'll find the closest place to land that's not too far from the entrance to the facility."

Charles leaned back and rubbed the condensation from his window. "There's something glowing on the right side back here."

"Ahh…there they are." the pilot maneuvered the craft as the landing lights and marshaller suddenly came into view. The landing skids sunk deep into the snow, and the propellers slowed down considerably.

The passengers had to use great force to push open the door against the wind. They stepped down into the deepness of the snow, and kept their heads far down as they moved towards the marshaller.

"Right this way, sir…the door is about thirty feet straight ahead."

the marshaller led the troupe as they trudged slowly toward the facility.

They huddled briskly through the outer doors, turned down the hall, and then into the operations room as the doors slid open. White paused by the door as he pulled off his parka. The howling wind of the blizzard was replaced by a warm rush of air brushing his cheek, beeping noises, and shuffling feet as he looked around the room. He removed the rest of his snow gear and handed it off. The soldier saluted him, and he returned the salute as he walked to the center of the enormous facility.

It was full of monitors manned by different military personnel in various positions placed strategically throughout the room. A radar type beeping continued at a steady pace. One officer was typing quickly, and to his left papers were strewn across a long table. The center of the main screen displayed a circular object appearing to have wings on each side and a trail of smaller objects behind it.

"What do we have here?" White pulled his glasses and handkerchief from his uniform's inner pocket, exhaled on and wiped both lenses, and leaned in for a closer look.

"Ohhhh…good morning, General." Colonel Bowdre saluted and pointed at the screen, moving his finger to the left and right of the planet. "All of these objects scattered about here mostly consist of space debris, along with a few comets and meteors, but all being pulled along by the magnetism of the planet."

An enlisted man walked up and stood stiffly next to the colonel, holding out a piece of paper. Bowdre paused as he took and studied the printout. "Very well, sergeant. Keep me posted," as he returned the sheet.

Another voice came from the lower right. "And don't forget…the planet has five moons, so some of those small blips could be a couple of those moons."

"That's right, Lieutenant…very good point." Bowdre's attention shifted back to the main screen.

"General, Colonel," one of the uniformed men named Jenkins turned, "you have to see this."

Both officers moved three stations to the right. Bowdre squatted down by Jenkins at his station, and White's eyes moved to the monitor, while some more men moved in around the station.

"There is a small blip in front of the planet." Jenkins put his finger by the object on his screen.

"Well, that could be one of the moons we've just discussed." Bowdre retorted.

"But sir…it moved."

The colonel paused for a moment. "Moved?"

"Yes, sir…moved. I've been tracking it for a while, sir."

"Let's put it on the big screen…let's see if we can get a better view." The group of men, now much larger with this latest discovery, moved left to view the huge main screen. "All right, Lieutenant Yates…let's increase the magnification and see what we've got here."

Everyone in the room studied the magnified image, but it was still too small and too distorted for anyone to make it out exactly.

"Could be an asteroid…" one voice said.

"Looks like a dead meteor to me," another man chimed in. "Notice there is no tail."

"Sir, now I'm picking up more blips on my monitor," Jenkins announced.

"Yes, I see them…they are moving into view now." Colonel Bowdre shook his head affirmatively as his eyes fixated on the screen.

As they zoomed in more, it became obvious to everyone what those objects in question were.

"These shapes seem to be a fleet of ships assembling in front of the planet, sir." Lieutenant Yates directed their attention by drawing a circle around the fleet's position on the monitor. "Because of their movement, there is no other explanation."

The Colonel turned to face his superior officer.

White clenched his jaw. Things just took a serious turn. The general turned to Lieutenant Yates. "How many?"

"Around fifteen, sir."

"Fifteen." The general rubbed his chin between his fingers and thumb. He stared at the enlarged screen. "We need to consider all of our options."

"Sir, I believe our main concern should be the vessels." Bowdre quickly turned to face him. "The formation of the fleet indicates a possible hostile stance."

"If I may interject..."

General White watched as Dr. Englestein maneuvered his way through the group to stand by Colonel Bowdre. "By all means, Doctor."

"I understand why this fleet of ships may be the prime and most urgent military concern, but from an astronomical standpoint, gentlemen...we have much bigger problems."

The general pointed at the screen, "What could be bigger than a fleet of enemy ships readying themselves for an attack here on Earth?" He grasped the rail in front of him, turned his head and listened intensely.

"I cannot argue with the urgency of this armada's possible attack on Earth, but much larger events of a catastrophic nature are looming in our foreseeable future." Dr. Englestein looked back and forth between White and Bowdre.

"Please continue."

"According to my calculations, gentlemen, this planet is traveling at an enormous speed, and has an elongated elliptical orbit with a thirty-three-degree tilt. This means if the planet stays on this same trajectory, and there is no reason for it not to do just that, the trek will place its orbit between the Earth and the sun-and even more precisely, Earth and Venus."

General White turned his head towards the screen and then back at the scientist. "You've got our attention."

"An object of this magnitude, approximately three times the size of Earth, traveling within such close proximity to our planet, could produce a number of cataclysmic consequences," Englestein took a deep breath, "including major earthquakes, multiple volcanic eruptions, serious climate changes along with species extinction." The doctor wiped his forehead. "Gentlemen...I am talking about a complete pole reversal."

Chapter Thirty

T.H.O.R.

"Thanks, Mom. The chicken was great," Lian put his napkin on the table, stood up, and looked down at his backpack. Some of the dark clothes he'd packed for tonight's mission were sticking out. He quickly shoved them in deeper and zipped the backpack.

"Cornish Quail." His mom smiled. "Now, to 'quail' in Cornwall still carries its old meaning, 'to shrink' or 'to wither.'"

Lian looked at her, pulling his head back and raising his eyebrows.

"The farmer dug his potatoes with all speed, and next year the almanac was richer by a score of subscribers."

"New cookbook?"

"Sir Arthur Quiller-Couch, *From a Cornish Window*."

"You never cease to amaze me, Mom," Lian said grinning.

She smiled, stopped for a moment, and looked at Lian. "And I am just amazed sometimes about how grown up you have become, right before my eyes."

"Well, I don't feel any different, Mom. I've got to go," Lian said as he leaned in to touch his forehead to hers. "Hey, maybe you're just in this reminiscing mood because we're *both* growing. While I'm growing up and looking at the future, you're growing older and looking at the past," Lian said with a bigger grin.

"Older?" his mom questioned.

"Well, I'm not saying you are old. I just mean …"

"I know what you mean," his mom cut in teasingly.

"Okay. Well, I'm off to pick up Gabriel, and shouldn't be too late."

"What is this for again, Lian?"

"Just some research, something we got from Professor Snodgrass today." Lian started to leave, then turned back around. "Be back soon...old lady."

His mom snickered as she watched Lian walk towards the side door. "You boys be careful."

"Alright, Mom. Love you."

"And I love you, son."

Lian walked to the car, and the door automatically opened for him. He climbed in, and put his backpack on the seat. "Good evening, Lian Hunter."

"Fila. I'm headed to Gabriel's tonight."

"Would that be Gabriel Stratus?"

"Yes, please."

"Gabriel Stratus – twelve point six minutes, ETA 5:48 P.M."

Lian sat back and thought about tonight's events. He thought about what he might find, if he could find anything at all on Lazarus Hunter. He also wanted to find anything he could on the statues they examined today. Who made them, who ordered them to be made in the first place, and maybe most importantly who designed them? Lian also thought leaving right after dinner would allow them enough time to find The Hall of Records, because it may be next to impossible to find such a mysterious building in the dark, even with the car's GPS and a map.

The screen lit up, and Fila's voice said, "Gabriel Stratus residence." Gabriel was waiting by his front door with his backpack. He walked over and the car door opened automatically once again.

"Got the map, right?"

"Right here, buddy. I looked it over quickly once I got home, and it looks like this Hall of Records *is* on the old academy grounds."

"Good. Fila, the old Tri-Asterisk Academy site."

A moment of silence, and Fila replied, "Old Tri-Asterisk Academy site–forty-six point three minutes, ETA 6:36 P.M."

140

Lian and Gabriel talked over how they would research the statues, and the possibilities of Lazarus Hunter being related to Lian. Each took turns at describing what the Hall of Records would look like, and what kinds of records the two of them would be able to access.

"Fila, let us know when we are getting close to our destination, let's say a few blocks from it, please." Lian instructed.

"As you wish, sir."

As Lian and Gabriel further speculated on the night unfolding, Fila announced, "Approaching Old Tri-Asterisk Academy site-five blocks ahead."

"Thank you, Fila. Now, slow down as we get closer. It'll be coming up on the left."

Lian opened his window and peered out, searching for the right building. This area seemed run-down, like an old metropolis that was very busy at one time, but now bore resemblance to an abandoned slum.

"Destination reached, Old Tri-Asterisk Academy site."

Lian looked out at the buildings. "This can't be right. Fila, a new destination, please, The Hall of Records.

The computer was idle for a few seconds. "Hall of Records, sorry, sir - no address matching that name."

"Maybe it is too old of a structure for the GPS." Gabriel guessed.

"Yeah, maybe. Gabe, let's get the map out and see if we can get our bearings."

Gabriel pulled out the map from his bag, unrolled it, and handed it to Lian. It was off-white, the sides and corners tinged a yellow color with some small tears on the edges. There was no date, just writing at the bottom of the map that said "Los Angeles, City of Angels."

His eyes scanned the map. The streets were laid out the same but many of the buildings were missing. The Hall of Records was labeled T.H.O.R. and was next to academic buildings on both sides that were now empty plots. The map showed a subway across the street from their target. Lian turned around and saw what looked like an old barricaded subway entrance behind them.

"Fila, let's pull up to that large chained link fence up ahead." The fence was surrounding some of the old academy buildings. Gabriel kept studying the old map, turning it from side to side and looking at it again and again, while looking outside at the actual site.

"That has to be it," Gabriel looked down at the map. "This map must be really old though because if you look right here where it says "Tri-Asterisk Academy," those buildings are missing." He held out the map to Lian. "See? Others are there, but…"

Lian looked across the street at an unmarked large grey building that had a rectangular shape and six large windows set high off the ground. "Well, there's only one way to find out," He handed the map back to Gabriel. They exited, and stood waiting by the car to cross the street as a few vehicles sped by in both directions. Lian raised his eyebrows as more traffic kept them from crossing. "Maybe we should have taken the subway."

"No thanks," Gabriel looked back at the subway entrance. "I'll take my chances with the speedy cars." They waited for the last one to pass, and finally ran quickly across the street. The last car blared its horn as it went by.

They walked up the steps and Lian pulled open the door. Once inside it looked like a library with long shelves of books. It had a musty smell like a tightly enclosed place covered in dust making it more difficult to breathe. He could not help but notice how different the place was from the Academy library, with its perfectly organized shelves that seemed to gleam against the polished floors.

Looking at the crowded book shelves laid out in a mishap fashion, Lian wondered how this place had any organization at all, and why it was still open for business. He concluded T.H.O.R.'s purpose was to store all of the historical documents, even if they were disorganized. The old linoleum floors with a mint green and yellow checkered pattern seemed to add to the confusion of the place. Straight ahead a woman sat behind a long counter piled with stacks of books.

"What should we say to her?" he asked Gabriel as they walked slowly toward her desk.

"Tell her you're looking for information for a book report."

Gabriel gave Lian a look as if asking a question more than giving an answer.

They walked up to the counter toward the woman. The way she sat between the piles of books reminded Lian of a mole. She had frizzy brown hair with beady black eyes. Her glasses seemed to almost teeter on the end of her nose as if they would fall off at any moment, but somehow managed to stay put. Her eyes darted from side to side while seemingly immersed in a large dusty book she was holding. She didn't seem to realize Lian and Gabriel even walked up and were now standing right in front of her. Lian looked at Gabriel for a sign he understood what was occurring, but Gabriel just shrugged and looked back at the woman. Her eyes continued to dart back and forth like a ping pong match over her book.

"Ahem. Excuse me, Miss," Lian said as he leaned forward. "Where would we find . . ."

Without looking up, the woman's high-pitched voice suddenly snapped, startling Lian and Gabriel. "All book areas are marked alphabetically." She moved her hand up and down rapidly as she pointed to the sign on the front of the desk stating the same message in big bold letters.

As both boys backed away from the counter, they saw the sign. Lian then looked around, but could not see signs anywhere.

"Well, what now?"

"Let's split up. I'll take the left side and you take the right." Gabriel frowned as he looked at the woman behind the counter. "Just let me know if you find anything, and maybe *I* can help. We sure can't count on anyone else around here."

Lian agreed, "See you in a bit." He stood there for a few minutes as Gabriel walked away. He had no idea where to begin, so he thought he would just start walking towards the farthest corner and make his way back towards the entrance. He looked at the books that seemed to be in more of a zigzag pattern than rows. He didn't understand why they would make a place intended for research so hard for people to find what they were researching. Then the thought crossed his mind that maybe they didn't *want* anyone to find anything. After all, the place seemed deserted except for Gabriel and himself.

He continued to walk between the long rows of books until he could not go any farther. Finally, he saw a small sign, which was placed up high in the middle of long shelf. He had to strain his eyes to read the small writing. *Pacts – Property*.

"Well, got to start somewhere." He thought to himself as he traced his finger along the shelf, scanning the book titles as he went from row to row. *Power of Practices, Presidents of the U. S., Property Protection.*

The more he looked at the titles, the more confused he was about where to look and what to look for. He grabbed the two outside books, thinking if he would skim through them, he might see something familiar. He blew the dust off the top cover of the book entitled *Property Protection,* and coughed a bit as he waved the dust out of his face. It was obvious no one had read these books in ages.

On the front cover was a picture of an estate with some statues perfectly arranged in the landscape. Lian remembered about the statues at the academy, and that he'd documented some of the information with some pictures. He paged through the pictures on his watch, and scrolled to the statues data. He thought of the statue and the list of names. Lazarus Hunter had to be someone very important to the academy, and even more pressing was the question how was he related. Lian looked at the rows and rows of books. Where should he start? Tri-Asterisk employees? He shook his head. Something did not ring right. Maybe it was because of the Hunter name. He could not picture anyone on his father's side as a professor or employee. He saw a sign on the side of one of the rows. *F-H...F-P.*

Founders. That was where he should start. He put the two books back in their proper place, and turned quickly down the aisle next to the F-H sign. Lian walked down one of the rows and again ran his finger across the top of books lining the shelf. Once more the dust rose up toward his face, reminding him of the frequency these books were read. Lian revisited the notion the lack of visitors and T.H.O.R.'s rather secretive location were exactly how the academy wanted things to be. It was a place where records were stored, but not meant to be seen. A building once part of the academy, but then discarded when a better, more private piece of land was purchased. This appeared to be in line with the way the academy and anyone connected with it thought, if you were no longer useful, you were dispensable, and you were discarded.

Lian saw only two books with the name "Founders" and pulled them both down to see if anything caught his attention. He sat down and leaned against the bookshelf. Quickly glancing side to side down the deserted aisle, he grabbed the first book and blew the familiar dust off the top cover. As the cloud lifted, the name *Founders of The Higher Order* became clearer. The opening page read *Articles of The Higher Order.* He continued down, the language had a long list of articles, propositions, and regulations. He was worried he would run out of time. The book was so thick it would take him a month to get through it. The dialog was also written in such a way, he was having a hard time deciphering what it was talking about. He flipped through the pages, suddenly stopping midway through when he saw a picture. A group of men were in a picture with the words *The Higher Order Founding Committee.*

He looked at the three rows of men all dressed in suits. He quickly scanned his eyes down below and saw the name *Lazarus Talon Hunter.* He looked at the picture above matching the order of the name. A handsome dark haired man stood in the front row. He recognized the dark eyes, the characteristic Hunter jawline. He had an intensity about him that was hard to describe. When he looked back to check the order in the picture, another name jumped out at him. *Octavius Rion Hunter.* He looked at the picture of the man whose eyes seemed gentler than Lazarus. There was something about Octavius, but Lian couldn't put his finger on it.

He continued flipping through the pages and stopped on another picture, seemingly not as old as the first. It appeared to be the same group of men posed in front of a banner displaying the same title, *The Higher Order Founding Committee.* This time he recognized a new face, the face of his grandfather. He looked down and saw the name *Phineas Darion Hunter.* His father was so secretive about his own father, and Lian hardly saw him at all before he passed away. Lian was five at the time, but he would never forget his grandfather's face. His mind drifted to one of the few times he visited him.

Lian knew Phineas Hunter was a man of few words, much like his father. He recalled he always had a scowl on his face, and never called Lian by his name, but referred to him as "the boy." Lian would be sent to play in another room when his father would be told to "Get that half-breed boy out of here so we can talk."

Eventually, Lian stopped accompanying his father on these visits. As much as he wanted to love and be loved by his grandfather, he realized even at such a young age, any reciprocation of those feelings would never come about. He didn't even know his grandfather had passed until he overheard his father and mother talking.

Lian thought for a moment, "*Get that "half-breed" boy out of here.*" Why did he not notice it before? With him being so young at the time, he didn't know what the term meant. However, what he did have were memories about his mom never associating with his grandfather. Even back then, Lian picked up on a very strong feeling his mother was the object of Phineas Hunter's dislike and mistrust. Another piece of the puzzle, and Lian was determined to solve it.

Lian was just coming out of these thoughts about his grandfather when his peripheral vision caught a person walking quickly by the end of the book aisle. He held the books under his arm as he walked slowly to the end of the book shelf and glanced around the side. When the figures came into view, he pulled his head back quickly so he would not be seen. Salem, Calek's older brother, was whispering back and forth with two other people, but Lian could not make out the conversation. *What are they doing here?*

He quietly set the books down on the shelf next to him, and moved a couple other books around so he could see what they were doing. He was barely able to see all three figures as they huddled together and continued their discussion. They were whispering too quietly for Lian to make any sense out of their conversation.

Lian began creeping slowly around the end of the bookshelf. He knew he had to find out what those three were up to. If Calek's brother was involved, he knew it couldn't be good. Lian raised up his panoptic watch through a gap in the books to take a picture. He lowered his arm back down and looked at the watch showing only an empty corridor.

"Huh? Where are they?" Lian whispered. He quickly stood up and looked through the books. They were gone. How could they have left so quickly? He would have seen them pass by. Lian lifted his head above the bookshelf, and moved it left and right, but saw no one. "I don't understand...unless there is a back exit door."

Lian walked slowly to the end of the aisle. Seeing the coast was clear, he crept over to where he had just seen them standing. No door. Nothing was there except a large wall with a crevice on one side. He ran his hand up one side of the groove and then the other, feeling for something that would create an opening of some sort. Like the opening itself, a lever, button, or switch had to be hidden, but had to be there somewhere. Lian knew he did not imagine them there one second and gone the next. Searching the area completely, he knew now there was no back exit door, so they had to go through a portal of some sort. He continued to run his hand up and down the wall as his eyes searched for some sort of button. He put his ear to the wall to listen, but didn't hear anything. As he put his eyes as close to the wall as possible to examine any differences in the surface, he noticed a small subtle panel about six feet off the ground and six feet from the corner. After looking it over carefully, he slowly raised his right hand, and placed his five fingertips on the center of the pane, and pressed in gently. Nothing. With his fingertips still affixed to the panel, he applied more pressure and heard a small rumble as a door near the end slid open. Moving in front of the opening, he saw it was very dark inside, but he poked his head in and slowly entered. He jumped and turned around as the door slid closed behind him. His eyes needed to adjust to the dark, and he listened, but couldn't hear Salem and his two friends. As his night vision improved, he could barely make out a set of stairs descending, but couldn't tell how far down they went. A small light on the wall lit up as his foot touched the first step.

Chapter Thirty-one

The Labyrinth

The stone steps curved around one way and then the other, and reminded Lian of a snake, a sidewinder making its way through the sand, slithering and gliding from side to side. When he reached the bottom of the staircase and stepped on the floor, the lights on the stairs went dim, freezing Lian. A huge chill went down his back as the lights went out completely, surrounding him in pitch black silence. Lian felt his breathing increase rapidly, fearing someone or something would grab him any second. Thinking it may be best to retreat at this point, he moved his right foot back onto the last step. Lian gasped and shielded his eyes as the staircase lights came back on at full intensity. He slowly pulled his hands down from his face, peeking between his overlapping fingers.

"So *that's* how this works." He moved his foot off the step and watched the lights dim once again, then placed it back on to see the bright change. Suddenly, a frightening thought ran across him as he looked up the stairway. He then looked left and then right down the corridors, making sure no one noticed his impromptu light show. He noticed there was no distinct difference either direction. *Think I'll go left. It looks brighter for some reason.* Heading slowly and nervously down the rocky tunnel, the staircase lights shut off, throwing him once again into complete darkness.

The walk felt slightly uphill for Lian, running his hand along the rocky walls, and as his eyes adjusted to the near-darkness, he noticed the corridor was getting brighter with each step. He realized a torch up ahead was lighting the way. He carefully peered around the corner of the next passageway to make sure no one was there. Still no sign of anyone, Lian searched the ceiling for any motion detectors or cameras that may be watching him. He did not see anything monitoring his movements. He found the torch, but it was much too high to reach, so he continued on.

Ahead of him and about half way down the next passageway, Lian spotted an opening, and moved closer to investigate. It was difficult to tell without the aid of light if this was another corridor or a room of some sort. The stone archway assured Lian it was probably a doorway to some room.

He entered the room and crept along slowly, spreading both arms as far as they would reach from side to side, and then moving them directly in front of him and then back again, his hands searching for any obstruction. The sound of small pebbles and rocks being kicked aside by his shuffling feet seemed unusually loud, so Lian thought taking small steps may draw less attention to his presence. His hands were outstretched as far as they would go to his side when his face ran directly into something sticky and musty. Lian let out a small gasp and pulled back quickly. He knew instantly he had run face-first into a spider web, a huge one spun from what probably was a huge spider. It encompassed his face, chest, and arms as he panicked and tried to pull away from the tacky substance on his body. The web constricted and jerked Lian forward, now capturing his lower torso and legs in the trap. He squirmed and turned, but nothing seemed to be working. He was finding himself more engulfed in the web with every movement. Lian suddenly stopped fighting to break free, took some deep breaths to slow down his heart rate, and started gathering all the logic and common sense he could muster.

Calm down, Lian...it's just a cobweb, quietly assuring himself as he gritted his teeth. "Just a little at a time..." he whispered as he took a small fistful of web and slowly pulled it off his face, and then removed it from his left side freeing his leg, "...and you'll be out of this mess quickly." He grabbed the remaining web and carefully freed his right side, finally managing to completely liberate himself from the entire sticky network. He took another step back from the large web. "Thank goodness the tenant wasn't home."

Backing out of the room, he continued down the single narrowing corridor. This way only got smaller and smaller and eventually came to a dead end. Lian grunted, turned and started back toward the staircase, blaming his instinct for not going to the right.

He was past the staircase now and heading downward through the passageways to the right. This way seemed to get more cavernous the farther he descended, and a distinct dampness in the air was evident on his skin. Lian's eyes kept adjusting to the near dark conditions between each of the torches placed high on the walls and spaced evenly throughout the corridors. They emitted just enough light to keep the tunnels from being completely dark. He still used his hands on the walls to navigate, and he noticed the stones were also gaining moisture as he kept descending. Lian came to a Y-intersection, and studied both tunnels trying to decide which one he should take.

This time he decided to travel to the right, and started moving slowly in that direction, again using his hands as guides. Lian immediately caught sight of another room. This one was on the right and luckily lit by a nearby torch. Examining the small room from the passageway, he could see this room contained nothing but an upturned mahogany table with three legs. Moving farther down he noticed the tunnel came to a T, which meant he had to make another split decision. Lian looked left but could not make out anything that way. Turning around and examining the corridor to the right, he saw nothing visible. He headed down the left tube. Just a few yards in, Lian tripped on a stalagmite and fell forward, catching himself, but scraping his hand on the rough surface of the stone floor. He used his left hand to check to see if his injury drew any blood. He felt wetness, but could not tell if it was blood or the residue from the damp walls and floor. He wiped his right hand on his pants and checked again. His hand was dry, but he could feel some abrasions on his skin.

Lian got up, brushed himself off, and walked on, this time taking smaller steps, carefully dodging any other stalagmites interrupting his trek. This tunnel was narrower than the other passageways he had encountered up to this point. The next torch revealed a wider path ahead.

As Lian slowly traversed the shaft, he picked up a faint sound up ahead, like water was running off a rock or coming out of a pipe and falling into a pool or stream of some sort. This dripping noise unconscientiously made him walk a little faster. He stopped again so he could listen and estimate how far ahead the water was from his present position. The sound was considerably louder, so he knew he was getting closer. Lian surged ahead and followed the turn through the darker passage, his left hand now navigating its way across the wet stones.

Lian was heading downward when his right foot suddenly failed to touch any ground. His left foot slipped forward, he fell back and his upper body hit the ground hard as he felt himself sliding forward over the edge. Lian yelped as he threw both hands to the wall to grasp on to anything resembling a ridge. He quickly found himself dangling over a cliff as his injured right hand caught a pocket in the side wall. Painfully swinging back and forth, he struggled to pull his body up to safety, desperately kicking his legs and trying to gain some footing on the side of the ledge. Gravel was falling all around him, and he could hear the rocks bouncing off different plateaus below him as he fought relentlessly to raise himself to safety. He moved his left hand into a similar pocket in the other wall, and started pulling himself up and over the ledge. Once he had his chest over the ledge, he dug the nails of his right hand into the floor, and hoisted his entire body to solid ground. Lian turned over on his back and hurriedly used both of his hands to push down and scoot his body back over the gravelly floor so it was far away from the opening.

It took a long while, but after Lian composed himself, he turned over on his stomach once again, got up on his hands and knees, and carefully crawled toward the ledge-his hands now using the floor as a guide. When he got to the edge, he laid flat on his chest and jutted his head forward to look down at what was below the drop-off. It was very dark to the right, but to the left he saw rays of sunlight coming down from various holes in the ceiling. Lian studied the area, and the scene in front of him started making sense to him. As he continued to survey the landscape below him, he was now able to distinguish the different shapes from one another, and make out what was left of some buildings about halfway up the opposite wall. This was the site of the old subway system. Some subway cars were turned over on their sides, and rails were piled on top of one another. Many were standing on end and leaning against the passenger platform. Water formed a lake where the normal tracks would have been running. Lian concluded an underground stream probably caused the subway system to fail at this particular location, not to mention the earthquakes. It was still an eerie sight with the rays of sunlight peering through, lighting up the ruins, and reflecting off the different pools of water.

Lian backed up, scooting on his stomach until he was certain he was well away from the edge. He stood up, and started making his way back through the tunnel. When he reached the intersection, he crossed over to the right side this time, again paying close attention to the floor for any impeding stalagmites he may encounter. There was still plenty of darkness between the torches, and Lian reasoned they were purposely spread that far apart so one would have to be familiar with the route to feel safe walking through it. He was starting to realize how far he was immersed in this maze. There was still no sign of anyone else in the tunnel system, but he had no choice but to keep going now. He just hoped he could find his way back out. He could feel the pulse of his heart and it was pounding in his ears as he carefully moved forward, keeping close to the wall. He wished Gabriel was here, and started to second guess his decision to follow the mysterious trio of boys without telling him.

Lian looked around, and saw another corridor up ahead. This tunnel had no torches, but a green luminescent glow instead. He noticed another opening in the wall farther up, but his mind was taking in the odd aura of the entire new passageway he'd uncovered. There perched up high on the walls were rocks-the source of the colorful light. He'd seen these rocks before. Snodgrass had the same ones in his classroom, except *these* specimens pulsated in and out, dim and then bright, almost like they were alive. Lian had to squint to search further down the passageway, and he was starting to feel dizzy from the strobe-light effect of the rocks. He knew he may have to find some places in this well-lit stretch of the maze to duck in and hide in case someone happened upon him.

He walked a little farther and came upon the opening he had seen when he first made the turn into this passageway. It was a room filled with shelves of these luminous rocks. These specimens were only slightly glowing, which made Lian wonder what the difference was between the two kinds. Just as he started to move into the room to get a closer look at the rocks, he picked up the sound of some people talking farther down the tunnel, but couldn't distinguish how far the voices were in the distance. He moved toward the talking, being ever so careful not to make a single sound.

Through the green glow he could see the walls were becoming even more like a cavern, like a tunnel in a cave made entirely of damp existing rock. It was much different than some of the walls and floors at the beginning of the corridor that were definitely man-made with carefully placed pieces. He kept his hands on the moist wall as he moved along slowly, mostly for stability. The green light was still creating a dizzying effect on him, even though he was moving away from that section of the cavern.

Lian suddenly heard a scurrying noise…someone or something was coming. He noticed a crevice in the wall to the right, small, but large enough to accommodate him if he slid in sideways. He quickly pressed his body into the crevice. As he faced outward he saw a shadow running past him, followed by a flash of a dark reddish brown object-maybe the size of a medium-sized dog. It hurried past…right in front of him. He breathed a sigh of relief as he recognized the figure. It was a bulldog rat, and its large body scurried off with its thick short tail trailing behind it.

He had to keep going, to keep moving a little faster toward the trail of voices getting fainter with every step. Lian's eyes scanned the walls as he descended deeper and deeper into the maze. The passageways were becoming colder and darker, and the only light now was coming from the next round of torches, also strategically placed high on the walls. He knew he had to act fast and walk even faster or possibly lose the opportunity to find the voices he heard. He needed to follow them to see if they would somehow lead to revealing at least part of this mystery. Lian hoped to have made some sense by now about what this labyrinth was hiding, but nothing was adding up for him.

A loud noise, a movement of some kind that seemed to slightly vibrate the entire underground system stopped Lian dead in his tracks. He couldn't exactly place the noise, couldn't imagine what object could shake the entire network of tunnels like that. Then the voices went silent, and he stopped walking to tune in to any trace of conversation. Was he too late? He listened for a very long minute, and then picked up the pace to try and reach the source that had gone silent.

He stopped suddenly when he heard more footsteps. This was definitely the sound of one or more people coming. He dodged into another nearby opening along the wall, this one a little deeper than the first. Lian heard the same loud vibrating sound as before, as two hooded figures in long red cloaks passed right by him. Luckily the hoods of their cloaks hid Lian from any side glances they would have taken, but unfortunately the hoods hid their identity as well. As they moved past the crevice Lian tried to hold his breath, but the harder he held it, the more it fought to be released. He stood frozen, waiting until they were well past him and the sound of their gait was inaudible. He exhaled, slid out of his hiding place, and hurried in the direction from where the figures had come. A large boulder doorway started to close, and Lian now knew this was the loud rumbling sound he had heard earlier…the door from which the two cloaked men had emerged.

Leaning forward and looking inside to make sure no one else was standing close or coming out, he quickly slid through the opening. His whole body shook as the door shut loudly behind him. If he had not just gone through the doorway, he would not be able to tell where it was, because the rocks making up the door fit perfectly into the wall like the last piece of a jigsaw puzzle. Lian was breathing harder now, and he could feel his entire body shaking from nerves this time. There was no turning back now. He needed to find a way to stay undetected in this lair. Another room or crevice would work, but he had to act quickly to find something to hide his presence.

Once he had stepped inside and controlled his seemingly loud breathing, he could hear the sound of voices again. Faint conversations, but definitely many more of them this time. Lian urged himself forward against the will of his body's own survival instinct. He encountered an open closet area, and when Lian examined it, he discovered boxes upon boxes of red robes. These were the same type of robes he saw on the two men who walked by him earlier. He moved a few steps to the right to another opening. This was a small round room, and he carefully stuck his head around the corner of the doorway so he could get a glimpse of what was inside. It was empty, except a large stone slab resting against a wall with a table next to it. It seemed like this ceremonial area of the cavern had the same dim green glow he saw in the room containing the shelves of pulsating green rocks.

As he passed the stone slab, he noticed the stainless steel table had a few red robes folded on top of it. On the far side of the table, his eyes picked up what appeared to be a closed closet door. As Lian walked up to the door, he thought he heard a noise coming from inside. He stood motionless in front of the door, his head turned slightly to pick up any other noises coming from inside the closet. He then put his hand on the doorknob and turned it very slowly until it would not turn any farther. Readying himself in a defensive position, Lian swiftly swung the door open. Red robes hung in front of him, and more were stacked on the upper shelves. Lian laughed quietly at himself for being so frightened at robes in a closet. Suddenly, a hand was on his shoulder and turning him completely around. A red-cloaked figure now faced Lian and had both of his hands on Lian's arms.

"What are you doing?" a deep rough voice emerged from underneath the robe. Lian could only make out a mouth as it asked again. As his inner strength grew rapidly within him, Lian answered with a swift blow to the figure's face, and the man fell backwards, taking Lian with him to the floor. Lian quickly rose up, and rapidly hit the figure four more times in the head. The man lay motionless. As Lian's anger and strength began to subside, he got up and ran to the door to see if anyone else had heard the skirmish. No one was in sight or coming to investigate. He looked to the left and saw more robes, thrown on the floor like a big pile of laundry. Without even thinking, he pulled the unconscious man across the floor to the pile, threw some robes on top of him, grabbed one of the garments from the table and slipped it over his head. The robe draped heavily around his feet, lying puddled on the floor. Lian pulled the hood up over his head, and it draped down so far, he could not see any more than two feet above floor level.

Feeling secure this incident and his identity remained hidden, he exited the round room, and started exploring the rest of the corridors in this section. Voices were growing louder, escalating as he moved farther down one of the passageways. He couldn't make out what was being said, so he continued walking, his robe dragging on the floor around him. As he got closer, it became obvious the conversations had now turned into chants, drone chants like one would hear in a monastery, completely in unison and repeated over and over. He moved into the large ceremonial room, and began seeing the bottoms of many robes, all moving slowly, all moving in cadence with one another. As he joined the ranks of chanters, he realized he'd walked right into the thick of the action. Lian felt like he was in a den of lions that hadn't seen him as their next meal yet. This thought made his heart pound even faster.

Then he heard it for the first time, a loud guttural scream coming from a girl. It was a scream of terror, accompanied by grunts and moans, and he could tell she was fighting to get loose from whatever was holding her. Normally, Lian's instinct would be to run toward the voice to help this girl, but this was not a normal situation by a long shot. He knew he had to keep his identity hidden while keeping this slow pace with the rest of the hooded figures. He continued toward the voices and the girl's panicked sounds of struggle. There was a heavier glow of green slowly pulsating all along the floor in this room. As he moved, Lian had to glide across the floor instead of walk to avoid tripping over the folds of his robe.

The chanting became louder as the men surrounding him joined the chorus. Lian could only see red robes, and then only from the waist down. The voices were echoing which made it difficult to estimate how many people were actually in this huge room, but Lian guessed the number to be at least one hundred from the chorus of voices. The monotone chant continued, "Azu...lavee...koratum," repeated over and over, sounding like a mantra...a transcendental meditation chant. The same words were repeated robotically...again and again.

Lian could still hear the girl, but the grunting changed to a muffled whimper as the rattling of a chain cut through the air. He was close enough now to get a fleeting glimpse of the girl, but his vision was blocked by row after row of red. He moved just enough to quickly catch sight of some wisps of blond hair just barely visible through the wall of cloaks. He wondered who the girl was and why she was here, but at the moment he had more important things on his mind, such as how he was ever going to get out of this situation. He could feel other men moving closer to him, and the ranks getting tighter as they were ushering into the room. Lian's heart was racing, and his breathing was so heavy now...so heavy he was sure someone next to him would be able to hear his nervousness. He started chanting with them, thinking it may disguise his abnormal breathing.

"Azu...lavee...koratum..." Lian started repeating the chant as he looked around. "Azu." He wondered where he had heard this word before. In fact, all three words were familiar to him, and it finally came to him. These words were all derived from the language of Sumer. As he continued chanting, Lian tried to see the girl's face and what they were trying to do with her, but all he could make out was she was barely clothed in a flowing white veil and secured on top of a slab of rock. This was a sacrificial stone. He chanced a quick step to his left, and finally saw her face. Lian knew this girl. Gabriel had recently sent a picture of her to his computer, and her smile in that photograph now flashed through his mind. She was one of the missing girls Jimmy mentioned at lunch that one day...Kate Faris. Lian had to figure out a way to save this girl, but what could he do when there were so many followers and only one of him? No doubt he would probably face a similar deadly fate. He stood paralyzed, his robe felt tight around him. His head was now throbbing. Lian knew even if he was able to get out of here and find help, it would be too late. He was not even sure he could navigate his way back to the staircase through the maze of corridors.

Just then his eyes picked up small glimpses of a larger figure in a black robe moving through the waves of chanting men towards the girl. Lian reasoned this had to be the leader of this crowd, at least to some degree. The red robes parted ceremoniously into a small circle as the leader approached the girl. The attention was centered on the elevated slab and the girl who struggled against the chains attached to it. The cloaked figures closed ranks and encircled the stone behind their leader. Lian moved his head slowly to the side to peer around the sea of red in front of him, and suddenly realized he was on the end of a perfectly formed row in the many columns of red fabric.

Lian again tried to take in as much of the room's atmosphere as he could. The green luminescent rocks continued to vibrate their hue in the room, and he could see some sort of statue bases, but could not see exactly what they were because the hood of his cloak hung so low. He had a suspicion these were the same statues garnishing the entrance to Tri-Asterisk Academy, but couldn't tell for certain. Suddenly the rows of red went down to a kneeling position, and Lian quickly followed suit. He could now see what developed at the center slab, as the only one standing was the leader in his black robe. This figure had climbed onto the ledge surrounding the rock slab. The leader loudly repeated the chant three more times, followed by three incredibly long and low-registered "Ommms." He then reached up with his left hand and lowered the black hood, exposing a bald head. The right hand shot up in the air and revealed a ceremonial dagger of some sort. Lian pulled his hood back slightly so he could see who this leader was. At first he thought it was the glow of the rocks making the bald head appear green, but then soon realized he was mistaken. As the leader sanctimoniously looked around the entire room at all of his followers, Lian recognized the other features, the scales, the large eyes, and the curled-up mouth. This was one of the statues. This *was* the Ensi.

Lian knew he had to get out of there. He had no choice, he was going to have to make a move, and it had to be now. He couldn't breathe.

The lump in his throat grew more and more painful. Luckily he was on the end of a row, and he thought he may be able to slip out without too much attention being drawn to him. As he slowly moved into the aisle, and turned around, he noticed everyone was bowing their heads. They didn't see him at all. He stepped quietly and quickly past the rows of red robes, making sure he moved one foot behind the other so he wouldn't trip. For a moment Lian thought for sure he was going to pass out. He turned back to the room, moving quickly toward the entrance, nearly hyperventilating when he almost stumbled over the back of his robe. He moved toward the open door, and before he could exit the room, the chanting grew louder and louder, until the worst sound he had ever heard in his life echoed off the walls. A scream of torturous pain and blood-curdling agony boomed through the cavern. He froze, the pulsating lights were flashing-almost like a heartbeat. She was gone and he couldn't help her.

Lian felt sick, he felt faint, and he tumbled against the cavern wall. He grasped to cover his ears as the chanting inside grew even louder, wanting it all to stop. Lian moved forward to his knees, but quickly rose up, his legs suddenly taking over as his body's own willpower urged him to escape. He just witnessed a girl being sacrificed by this evil cult, and there was nothing he could do. He felt like he was going to get sick again, but he knew he had to finish this.

Once he was completely out of sight, he struggled to get through the door and back into the room, and he pulled off his robe and threw it aside. *This girl's death must be avenged,* he thought. He looked up at one of the torches on the wall, and suddenly met with an epiphany. *That's it. Fire. The catacombs were destroyed by fire.*

He quickly picked up his discarded robe, and hurried into the adjoining room where he had first gotten it. He grabbed all the robes on the table and floor and rushed out of the room. He then rushed into the closet area. He was feeling stronger and thinking clearer now, and knew what he had to do to avenge the girl's gruesome death. He threw the robes in his arms into one of the boxes and carried it to the outside room, and quickly ran back to gather the rest. Lian piled the robes on top of the boxes in the only corridor leading to the ceremony room. The pile was over four feet high, and stretched the entire width of the entryway. He climbed up the pile and grabbed both torches off the wall. He quickly placed the torches near the bottom of the pile, and the robes immediately caught fire. Smoke billowed upward, and Lian could tell these were multi-synthetic cotton robes that would burn for a long time, long enough to create a deadly smoke-filled ceremonial room. No one would be able to extinguish the huge blaze. No one would be able to breathe, much less open the boulder to escape and pass through the fiery barrier. Lian was confident most, if not all of the cult members would perish from smoke inhalation…a well-deserved fate for these evil souls.

Lian pushed the lever, and as the boulder swung open, he hurried through and ran as fast as he could in the opposite direction, trying to retrace his steps to the stairs leading to the Hall of Records. He turned to look behind him, the fire now filling the ceremonial room with smoke as the boulder slammed shut. All kinds of questions were running through his brain as he was running for his life through the passageways. He wondered if he just witnessed a Sana Baba ritual…he'd heard that term somewhere before. Was the leader a real person in a mask, or was it actually the statue that had come to life? Was this the same one Gabriel and he had seen on top of the pyramid, the Ensi? It all seemed to be linked, but he could not put it all together. His mind was becoming more confused with the fear running through his entire body. He had to concentrate on getting out of this maze…back to Gabriel to tell him what happened.

He quickly passed through the glowing rock corridor, and headed for the intersection. When he reached it, he continued straight down a passageway as it wound around into other tunnels. Realizing he had gone the wrong way, and he had taken a wrong turn somewhere, he knew he could not afford to make another mistake. Lian reached out in the darkness, his lungs burning from his heart racing. "Where am I?" He grasped at the nothingness in the air. His hand suddenly glanced off something sharp, and he could hear echoes of voices behind him in the distance. Lian suddenly realized he was actually living his recurring dream. He looked down at his panoptic watch to use the compass setting, but the hands just spun erratically. He was running out of time, but he had to keep his head clear enough to retrace his steps and remember which turns to make that would take him back to the staircase. Lian turned around and headed back the other way. When he got back to the T he turned left. He eventually came across the stalagmites he had tripped over earlier, and it occurred to him the journey back was much harder to recognize. When he came to the next intersection of tunnels, he stopped and calculated which way he should proceed.

The faint smell of smoke had already reached him, so he knew he had to hurry and be precise in his navigation if he was to get back to the Hall of Records safely. The walls were becoming more smooth and man-made in structure, which told him he was running in the right direction in the corridor leading to the exit.

Lian ran non-stop until he was back at the stairway leading to the entrance. As soon as his foot touched the first step, the staircase lights came back on. He was spent, but he ran as quickly as he could up the steps. His feet moved so fast, he slipped once, but got back up, and started taking two and three steps at a time as he made his way back up the winding staircase to the entryway from the Hall of Records where he began. When he got to the top, his hands searched all over the wall until one of them hit a hidden lever and the door slid open. Out of breath and feeling faint again, he started to doubt what he saw. The door began closing on its own accord, as Lian scrambled through it. He slid across the floor, tried to get to his knees, but then landed on his side. He was now in a powerful daze, and everything was spinning. He wanted to call out for Gabriel, but could not make any sound. Lian was nearing unconsciousness when suddenly someone grabbed his arm.

"Let's get you out of here," Gabriel commanded.

"It was real, Gabe. It was real." Lian gasped as he felt himself fading into black.

Chapter Thirty-two

Snodgrass

Two cups with their respective saucers found their way through the warm water and suds to eventually clink the bottom of the sink. Professor Snodgrass rinsed the gravy from his plate, and then stood for a minute and watched as the matching plate took the same back and forth path to join the other submerged dishes. The Salisbury steak and mashed potatoes were more than adequate for tonight's meal. They were easy to warm up in the microwave, and even easier to eat. He usually kept the kitchen in fairly decent order, compared to the rest of his traditional style house, and this was made easier because he used the same eating utensils daily. He would eat and drink from the glass and plate, clean them, leave them in the dish drainer, and then use them again for the next meal. He felt he should move on with his work now, and come back and take care of the dishes later after they have soaked for a while.

He normally kept the radio on every hour during the day, if he was there or not, and it was always tuned to the same station with the same talk shows. Tonight was different. He turned the radio off. He needed to think. Some problems swimming around in his head for a few days have recently started to swim closer to the surface, and he needed to sort out the details.

The professor moved to his office, which was really an extra bedroom. Fairly small with a large roll-top desk sitting by the window, Snodgrass's office gave off a feeling of compactness that would drive your average claustrophobic screaming out of the room in just a few seconds. Although he found the closeness of the walls of this confined space to be a secure and comforting haven to concentrate. He had a huge assortment of books and papers at his disposal. Some were very neatly arranged in the bookshelves, but in direct contrast, the majority of them were disheveled along the floor, on chairs, and on the desk. Many of the items in his collection had improvised bookmarks, such as napkins, pencils, and even other periodicals sticking out of the tops and bottoms. One huge binder even had a tail of some poor creature protruding out to mark his place. This was typical of the professor's filing system. There appeared to be no rhyme or reason to his method, no sense of order in the piles of publications, but Snodgrass knew exactly where every scrap of information was located in his office, and could retrieve it in a matter of seconds. He sat down in his chair, swiveled it around to face the large bookshelf stretching to the ceiling, and leaned back as far as the chair would allow. His eyes were determined to fixate on every book in every row of every shelf from top to bottom, time and time again if necessary, to retrieve the link he required to finish the enigma he faced.

"It's here. I know it's here. I also know this has to be a three or four step process in a precise order to arrive at the answer I seek," he told himself. "But, it's here. I just have to put it together."

Snodgrass eyed the various titles in his bookshelf. Although most were too far to read the actual titles, he could tell what they were from their covers. On his eye's second trip down the huge book shelf, he started counting how many of each color he had, how many books were short and tall, thick and thin in his collection. He scanned stacks of journals and newspapers, any kind of pattern or progression that might stir his thoughts. If he could clear his mind by thinking of something else while still in the presence of the books, he could possibly find the key to jumpstart his brain to the solution.

The professor removed his glasses, closed his eyes, and massaged his tear ducts around the bridge of his nose for a few seconds. He stopped rubbing as he heard his huia bird Donner start singing. He looked over at the bird in its huge cage, and gazed at its long curved beak and striking black feathers. The bird stared back at the professor, and again remarked, "Uia, uia, uia." Donner's song was soothing to the professor, and at times he would carry on a conversation with the bird, asking him a series of questions in a higher register as most people do with their pets. Sometimes its shriek got so loud, it would drive Snodgrass racing through the house to cover the cage with a black sheet to silence it. At night Donner was a different sounding bird as he would sing softly, especially when he was hungry. The professor thought this nightly song sounded like he was asking "Where are you?" The bird was appropriately dubbed "Donner."

"You are singing to me. Are you hungry, my friend?" Snodgrass inquired of the bird. "Let me get you some more food and water for your cage while I am thinking about it."

The bird was soon feasting on some seeds and grains with ground-up insects. Every once in a while he would let out a small gargling sound, almost like a purr. As Snodgrass opened the compartment for the water, it hit him.

"Water...*yes*." He immediately went to his desk, and started scratching out his notes. "This was so simple. I don't know why I didn't think of it sooner." He frantically wrote down line after line, pausing ever so often to tap the eraser part of his pencil on his lip. At one point when he wanted to accent an important part of his work, he pressed down so hard on the paper that the lead broke. He simply turned to the corner of his desk, pushed his pencil a couple of times into his top-of-the-line electric sharpener, and continued again on his notes. Snodgrass worked nonstop for another fifteen minutes, quietly dictating to himself as he turned sentences into paragraphs. Then he stopped abruptly, carefully laid his pencil down on his work, stood up straight, and walked into his kitchen.

The professor grabbed the tea kettle from the stove, filled it with water, and returned it to the front burner. He watched in silence as the flames climbed up around the kettle. He was thinking of water, and how that was the key to his thought process.

The phone rang, and the professor walked across the kitchen to answer it.

"This is Professor Snodgrass."

As the voice on the other end of the line talked, the professor seemed to concentrate on every word, his eyes shifting left and right.

"I see." After a few more seconds of listening, he spoke again, "I see. And you are quite sure this happened today?" The voiced continued on for another minute. Then in an exchange of rapid questions and answers, Snodgrass softly inquired "Anyone hurt? Mm-hmm. Were there any witnesses? Do you have a name or two? I see. Yes, thank you for your call. Please keep me informed."

He turned around to check on the water for the tea, and the phone rang again.

"This is Professor Snodgrass."

"Professor, this is Gabriel. I need your help. We're in trouble here."

"Gabriel, where are you?"

"We are behind the Hall of Records building. Lian is hurt. Can you please come get us?"

"I'll leave now. I shall be there in ten minutes."

"Thank you, Professor. I had no one else I could call."

"It's all right, Gabriel. Stay hidden. I will be there as soon as possible."

"Okay. Thank you, Professor! Thank you."

Snodgrass quickly turned the burner off, moved the kettle across the stove, grabbed his keys from the key holder by the backdoor, and headed outside to his car.

Chapter Thirty-three

The Reptilians

Lian awoke with a start, gasping as he sat up. His eyes quickly refocused on Gabriel sitting next to him. "Where are we?" He looked around the room.

"Relax, Lian. We are in Professor Snodgrass's house." Gabriel was treading cautiously, trying to choose the right words. "You blacked out."

Lian began studying his surroundings, and realized he was on a tan sofa, a few mismatched pillows were propped up behind his head. It was a small cramped living room with various papers strewn about. He noticed a stack of framed dark parchments sitting unhung against a wall. A few masks leaned against the opposite wall, propped unevenly against each other. The whole house had an unfinished feeling, like someone who procrastinated and left the smallest projects undone. He looked at a blank wall to his right. A dark red color was brush-stroked in one place on the wall as if to test the color. Lian's eyes caught sight of the book shelves across the room lined with some artifacts similar to the ones in Snodgrass's classroom and placed between some old books. He saw a light green rock sitting on one of the shelves, just like the ones in the labyrinth. Some things started coming back to him. His heart began to pulsate as he thought of the missing girl's cries and the enraging fire.

Professor Snodgrass entered the room carrying a large tray with a teapot and two cups. A licorice smell wafted through the air from the steam emitting from the teapot.

"Good to see you've joined us again," Snodgrass leaned down to set the tray on the table.

Lian noticed the professor's hands were shaking as he poured the tea, and one of the tea cups was too full while the other had more tea on the saucer than in the cup itself. Snodgrass took a step back from the table and sat down in a dark green wingback chair across the room. Lian continued to watch the professor fidget in the chair for a moment, then sit back and lift his leg, crossing it over the other.

Gabriel reached forward and picked up the overflowing tea cup, carefully holding the saucer underneath it. "Thank you Professor," he said, leaning forward and sipping the hot tea.

A melodic "Uia, uia, uia" carried through the air.

"Is that the huia bird you've mentioned before in class, Professor?" Gabriel inquired.

"Yes, that's him. That's Donner."

"Donner?" Gabriel asked.

"Well, I didn't name him. His original owners gave him that moniker. Although they did tell me he was named for the Donner Party."

Gabriel thought for a moment, and asked, "You mean *The* Donner Party, the pioneers who were trapped by snow, some eventually resorting to cannibalism to survive?"

"Yes, the very same. Remarkably *this* Donner was also found in the snow, where he must have escaped from his owners somehow. For a bird native to New Zealand, surviving even a couple hours in the snow is miraculous. He was nearly frozen when they found him, so that is where he got his name."

"Very interesting." Gabriel raised his cup to his lips and blew on his tea once again.

"Yes, I always thought so." Professor Snodgrass and Gabriel simultaneously started sipping their tea.

An uncomfortable stillness filled the room, but Lian's thoughts kept him quiet as they were swimming uncontrollably in his head. He was trying to decipher the meaning of everything he saw, running it over and over in his mind like a broken record. *What did it mean? Was he just imagining things?* He looked over at Gabriel and Professor Snodgrass who were both studying him. *Were they in on this too? Could they be trusted?* Lian looked at Gabriel wrestle a bit with the teacup to take another sip, and suddenly felt bad for even thinking such a thought. This was his friend, and they have been friends for as long as he could remember. As far as Professor Snodgrass was concerned, he was always trying to help them. Lian knew he had to pull himself together, and steer clear of any paranoia concerning tonight's events if he was going to figure out what actually took place.

Professor Snodgrass cleared his throat, breaking the silence in the room, and then spoke. "Lian, why did you go down under the Hall of Records?"

Lian looked over at Gabriel as if to gain more confidence. "I saw Salem, Calek's older brother, walk by me when I was looking up information about my family. He was with two of his friends, and they were whispering something." Lian felt an ache in his throat-a painful pressure building up when he swallowed and spoke. "I could tell something was going on, so I moved in closer to listen in on their conversation, but they suddenly started walking toward the back of the Hall of Records. I stayed hidden, but when I moved forward to eavesdrop on them again, they were gone…almost as if they had disappeared."

Lian looked back and forth between Gabriel and the professor who were both listening intensely. "I thought I'd lost them. I first looked for a rear entrance to the hall, then examined the entire area where I saw them last, and the only thing that made sense was they disappeared near that spot, perhaps behind the nearby wall. I started looking for some kind of mechanism that would reveal a door." Lian began moving his hands and acting out the scenes as he related them. "I ran my hand all over the surface of the wall, but couldn't feel anything unusual. When I put my ear to the wall listening for any sounds, I noticed a raised panel…so I pushed on it. That is when a door in the wall slid open. The next thing I knew, I was standing in a dark passageway at the top of some stairs, and the door was closing."

The room started to grow quiet again. Gabriel sat up straight in his seat and Professor Snodgrass had leaned forward, his chin resting on his hand with his elbow propped up on the arm of the chair.

Lian continued, "It was very dark, but I could make out the steps curving down. I thought maybe they would lead to the old subway system." He looked over at Gabriel, "Remember? We saw it across the street before we went in there. I thought I might have heard voices, but I wasn't sure. A light came on as soon as I took the first step, so I followed the staircase down."

Lian went on to explain his exploits in as much detail as he could muster. "Parts of the tunnel were lit up with these green rocks, like the ones you have up there on that shelf. But these rocks were glowing...bright then dim, and bright again."

Snodgrass turned to look at the shelves, "Those are rocks I collected on one of my digs in Turkey. I've never seen them pulsate, or even glow for that matter. They are indeed *old*, but they are found in great quantities in many ancient sites." He cleared his throat, and took another sip of his tea. "But please...go on, Lian."

Lian paused as he thought about how disoriented and dizzy he had become from the strange rocks. He moved on to the most important topic- the hooded figure he had seen during the ceremony.

"There is more." Lian recounted all of his exploits in the labyrinth, and at times he had to stop to compose himself. He would put his hands over his face, rubbing them up and down as if he could wipe away everything he had seen and every emotion he had felt. "Over a hundred of them...over a hundred cloaked figures." Lian's eyes tinged with tears as he re-lived the horrible sounds of the girl crying and then screaming. Suddenly Lian was not able to control his emotions any longer. He started crying, rocking back and forth as he grabbed a handful of hair in each of his fists. "They had a girl...one of the missing girls. It was Kate Faris, I remembered her. And I didn't help her. I *couldn't* help her. I just couldn't, you understand?" Lian cried harder, but this time silently into his hands as his head fell forward.

Professor Snodgrass got up and left the room. He returned with a damp washcloth. "Here, son, take this." The washcloth felt warm as Lian buried his face into it, wiping the tears and holding the warmth against his eyes.

"Are you able to continue, Lian?" The professor sat down in the armchair and swiped his hands over his knees to dry them.

Lian nodded as he put the washcloth on his forehead and stared at the ceiling. He was still trying to make sense of everything he had experienced. He let out a deep breath with the last detail of his night. "There. I said it." instantly feeling a tremendous sense of relief. It was as if he had just let go of the deepest, darkest secret ever.

Not a word was spoken for what seemed like an hour. Lian closed his eyes and tried to not think. He wished he could wake up and find all of this was just a nightmare.

Lian heard Snodgrass's chair scratch a little against the hard wood floor as he got up, and a rustling of papers and books being shuffled through. He opened his eyes and saw the professor was strategically looking through a large book. The book was so old the binder had come loose, and a few pages flew in the air and floated to the floor. The professor ignored the falling pages, licked his index finger, and quickly turned the pages.

"Here." Snodgrass walked over to Lian, sat the large book on his lap, and stood over him. Lian sat up straight on the couch, and Gabriel got up and sat next to him.

Lian's mouth fell open as he looked at the page. Drawings and diagrams of the green hooded figure were shown at different angles, and Lian's eyes couldn't scan the page fast enough. In every depiction he noticed the curled-up mouth and the scaly skin, and seeing those images gave him a sick feeling deep in his stomach. He looked at the opposite page, and the heading read "The Reptilians."

Lian looked up at Professor Snodgrass, "This is what I saw. I knew it was real." Again he felt relieved to know he was not losing his mind. He looked over at Gabriel who looked more shocked than Lian did.

"Yes, the reptilians are real. But, they have not been here for thousands of years. Still on Nibiru, we suspect." Snodgrass paused and took out a handkerchief to wipe a bit of sweat off his forehead.

The phone rang and each one of them jumped. The professor walked out of the room to answer it, Lian looked back down at the book.

He looked over at Gabriel, and looked down at the diagram again. "I knew I saw this. It was the Ensi we saw on top of the pyramid."

The professor returned to the room, "Gabriel, it was your mother. She said she's sent the car, and it will be here in a couple minutes."

"Thank you, Professor." Gabriel walked over and grabbed his backpack full of books. Lian slowly stood up, set the book down on the couch, and took one last look at the images staring back at him. He followed Gabriel and Snodgrass to the door and walked outside.

It was pitch black out now, except for the sliver of a moon hanging low in the sky. There was a soft breeze blowing, and Lian looked up toward the sound of the leaves rustling in the oak tree in the front yard. His attention then shifted toward a black car parked across the street a couple houses down. It looked as though the windows were tinted black, but Lian couldn't be sure. He suddenly got the feeling they were being watched. He looked over at Professor Snodgrass who also noticed at the car.

As Gabriel watched his family's car pull into the driveway, the professor looked over at Lian. "Are you feeling better there, my boy?"

"Much better, Professor, thank you. I think the book helped."

"Good. Well, off with you two then. Call me if you need *anything*." Gabriel climbed in and Lian followed. Snodgrass stood watching from his porch as they drove off.

Chapter Thirty-four

The Chase

Lian turned to look out the back window. The black car was still following them as they turned up the steep hill to his house. He looked over at Gabriel whose mouth twisted with worry.

"Maybe we should meet up at the Lost Cave." Lian suggested.

"Yeah, we need to figure out how to get rid of them." Gabriel gestured to the car behind them.

"If I can get to my four-wheeler, I think I can lose them." Lian was trying to sound as confident as possible as he looked at Gabriel. "You know, what worries me is they will know where I live, and I have put the safety of my family at risk, on top of everything else."

"Trust me, Lian...they already know where you live. And your family was already at risk when we started this adventure."

Lian looked at his friend, realizing there was an edge to the sound of his voice. Gabriel quickly unzipped his backpack and pulled out a large book.

"Is that from Snodgrass?" Lian guessed looking over at the book appearing to be very old by its cover and the condition of its binding. "No...you took that from The Hall of Records. Didn't you?" He could see from the expression on Gabriel's face he was right. "Why didn't you say anything before?"

"I didn't want Snodgrass to know I was stealing from The Hall of Records." A serious expression covered his face. "Remember...he trusted us with his map."

Both Lian and Gabriel looked out the rear window and saw the mystery vehicle put more distance between the two cars, but was definitely still following them. Lian moved in closer as Gabriel opened the book to reveal old news clippings. Both set of eyes strained to read the small print in the dark. "Dira, main passenger light please."

Light suddenly filled the car. Gabriel turned to the midsection of the book, and started rapidly flipping the pages. His finger found the page, and as it touched the article he looked up at Lian. The name Octavius Hunter jumped out.

Los Angeles Daily News

After a fourth day of searching failed to produce the body of LA resident Octavius Hunter, thirty-seven, Los Angeles County sheriff's homicide detectives said they are now categorizing his disappearance as a murder. They plan to interview his wife, Shala, thirty-five, after she reported that her husband was reported missing Saturday. Hunter did not return from a trip that he took near the Terranea Resort in Rancho Palos Verdes, authorities said.

Lian moved to the next page with the next clip, and his eyes widened even more.

The Los Angeles. Times

Lazarus Hunter, thirty-four, a resident of Los Angeles, was arrested on Wednesday, charged with the murder of his brother, Octavius Hunter, thirty-seven. Sources say there was a growing tension between the siblings which might have led to the murder.

"Lazarus murdered Octavius? His own brother?" questioned Lian, who nervously started shaking his head.

"It shocked me too. I knew you had to see this."

"What else could there be that would top any of this?" Lian looked deep into Gabriel's eyes for a possible answer.

"I can't say it gets any better, but look at this one."

Los Angeles Daily News

Lazarus Hunter, thirty-four, was released from the Los Angeles County Prison today. All charges have been dropped against Mr. Hunter regarding the murder of his brother Octavius Hunter, due to the lack of evidence. The Higher Order of Tri-Asterisk Academy was instrumental in demonstrating to the court that any evidence linking Lazarus to the murder of his own brother during the appeal was circumstantial or missing. Sources say that thus far there are no further leads in the investigation.

Lian's eyes now became as big as saucers, and as the two exchanged glances again, Lian blurted, "Are you thinking what I'm thinking?"

Gabriel turned and raised his head once again, looking back towards the headlights following them. "Sounds like someone was protecting Lazarus. Definitely the Higher Order of the Academy, but I think it goes beyond that…like someone or something very powerful."

Lian grimaced. His mind was racing again. How did Octavius die? Did Lazarus get away with the murder of Phineas' father? Was this why his grandfather was such a mean and unloving person?

"And look at this." Gabriel carefully turned the pages.

Lian was almost too scared to look. Were there more murderers in his family? His eyes narrowed as he looked down at the old type.

C. L. Hagely

The Los Angeles Times

Lazarus Hunter was awarded full custody of his nephew Phineas, two, son of Octavius and Shala Hunter, in a court decision today. The decision was not without controversy, since Lazarus Hunter was recently a suspect in the death of his brother Octavius. The charges were quickly dropped after an appeals court found that the evidence linking Lazarus to the murder had mysteriously disappeared. Lazarus was released from prison just two months ago. Octavius is also survived by his wife Shala, who has since disappeared.

"Phineas Hunter was my grandfather." Lian exclaimed.

"And he was raised by Lazarus," Gabriel added.

"No wonder my father didn't seem happy when I brought up the name Lazarus." Lian shook his head. He now knew his grandfather was raised by his uncle, an uncle who probably murdered his own brother, Lian's true great-grandfather. It all seemed like too much to take in...so many secrets. The information hit Lian hard because his hands slid over his face.

"Octavius seemed like a good guy." Gabriel patted Lian on the shoulder. "He seemed to be a humanitarian of sorts." Lian watched Gabriel as he paged back in the book and continued. "See what I mean? It says he was the on the board of many charitable foundations, he was chairman of the World Hunger Organization for two years, member of the Fair Trade Organization, contributed generously to Animal Rights, . . ."

"And a member of the Higher Order." Lian added in a disgusted voice.

"Yeah, but look here, Lian...not for long. It looks like he removed himself after one year. That's good, right? It also says many of the organizations he worked for opposed the policies of . . ." Gabriel paused as their eyes locked. "...everything Lazarus worked for."

"If nothing else, now we know the motive." Lian added. "Good brother versus bad brother."

"And at least *someone* was good in your family," Gabriel joked, trying to make light of the situation. "Let's face it, Lian. They don't all come across too well."

"Yeah, you're probably right."

"I know I'm right. The question now is what are you going to do about all of this?"

Gabriel's question hit home with Lian. It hurt, but it made him think hard about the possibilities. Just how far would these people take this? What harm could come to his family? He was sure of two things, he saw things that were not supposed to be seen, and he was going to stop any possibility of his family getting hurt.

"There is something else." Gabriel looked back at Lian sternly and put his right hand on his best friend's shoulder. "I think I've discovered something that will really surprise you. I'm not sure what it all means exactly, but it sure feels like there is a link, a connection. I wanted to mention this earlier, but these articles were revealing a lot of important facts about your family, and that took priority."

"What is it? Is it important?"

"I think that is something you can decide. When I was looking through some of these articles about your family, one of the names stuck out. I remember you telling me about your first day in the new observatory and the constellation that puzzled you, Orion. Remember?"

Lian's head shifted down and shook in agreement.

"Well, think about it. Octavius Rion Hunter…that is *O. Rion Hunter*."

"Orion the Hunter."

"Yeah. Is it just a coincidence he is named that, or is there meaning behind all of this?"

Lian thought for a few seconds. "Now I have even more to think about, like the stars aligning somehow with my ancestors, my family."

"Right now, I think we have bigger issues to worry about…like that car behind us."

Lian looked out the window. He saw the car and he could see his house up ahead. He could feel his heart pounding faster as they approached the driveway to his house. When he turned back around, he saw the car slow down and turn off its headlights as it parked down the street.

"Gabe, I could use your help, but I wouldn't blame you if you want to stay out of this."

"You're joking, right? Remember, I'm in this thing as deep as you are, my friend." Gabriel's hand landed on Lian's back. "There is no way you're doing this without me."

Lian smiled at Gabriel, and looked up at his house. The kitchen light was on and he knew his mother was waiting for him inside. He quickly opened the car door, giving Gabriel a knowing nod as he grabbed his backpack. Lian ran up to the front door of his house, pretending to open the door as he turned and waved as Gabriel's car drove off. It was very dark out except for the porch light casting a shadow on the ground. He looked out toward the street, and saw the wrought iron fence blocked most of the view. He knew they would be watching, and there was no time to waste. He ran around the house and opened the side door.

"Mom. I'm home, but I'm staying out here with Gabriel for a while."

"Okay, Lian. I am going to head up to bed then. Goodnight. Don't stay out too late."

"I won't. Goodnight, Mom." Lian laid his backpack by the backdoor and ran next to the side of the house toward the garage. He opened the side door and turned on a small work table light. His four-wheeler sat in the corner of the garage, partly covered in a light dust from his last ride. He switched off the light, quickly grabbed the handles of the four-wheeler and pushed it out through the side door. The weight of it was heavy but he could not risk starting it yet. Lian calculated if he could make it to the top of the small hill on the side of the house, then he could roll his bike much easier toward the road. He worried again about being followed, his eyes held steady toward the road. He tried to keep his footing as he leaned into the bike, pushing with all his weight. He couldn't see anyone ahead as he made it to the top of the hill.

"Now is as good a time as any," Lian jumped on the bike and turned on the ignition. The sound of the engine rang through the still air. He focused his thoughts on making it to the cave, and finding a way to lose the car along the way. Suddenly, he flew forward off his seat, realizing too late he'd slowly steered the four-wheeler into a hole. Lian grasped the handles tighter, struggling to regain control of the handle bars as the bike continued to jet forward. He'd just regained his balance when the tires grabbed the road, quickly picking up speed. A sharp pain shot through his chest where he had hit the wheel. He turned and saw the black car behind him still waiting. His heart jumped as the car's lights suddenly flashed on, blinding him. When he turned back around he had trouble seeing ahead, and the fog that rolled in made the visibility even worse.

Now Lian could hear the car getting close…so close he was worried it would hit him at any moment. He made a left turn at the next street, and now the car was right next to him. He quickly tried to see who was following him, but the tinted black windows only revealed the four-wheeler's lights. The car suddenly swerved toward him, and Lian instinctively pulled down on the wheel to avoid being hit.

His left tires were the only things clinging to the road when he saw his usual pathway to the beach just ahead. He reached it just in time as the car swerved towards him again. Lian jerked his vehicle sharply to the right, and headed down the narrow sandy path. The four-wheeler jolted up and down as it hit the mixture of sand and patches of grass. He knew the car would get stuck if it tried to follow him. He breathed a sigh of relief as the sound of the car faded behind him.

As he got closer to the ocean, an even heavier fog hung in the air. Lian strained his eyes as he tried to stay on the path, but his single headlight added very little visibility in the foggy dark. He winced in pain as he hit another small pothole lunging him forward again, this time hitting his jaw on the handle bars. Finally, he could make out the end of the path as he jetted left and picked up speed. As he continued riding, the fog lifted enough he could see the crescent shaped moon set low over the ocean, and the high tide produced sprays of water hitting his face as he went. He could hear some waves slamming against the rocks up ahead as he made his way to the opening of the cave. Gabriel was sitting on his bike by the entrance.

"Did they follow you?"

"They tried," Lian was panting hard and trying to catch his breath, "but I lost them at the main path." As he exhaled, he softly added, "They tried to knock me off the road with their car." He bent forward, his stomach was now in knots.

Both boys looked around, and suddenly zeroed in on the same spot. Four large hulking figures were approaching. The moonlight shown across them as Gabriel and Lian both let out a gasp. As the figures moved in, they began to spread out to surround Lian and Gabriel, one at each corner. They were all over six feet tall with large eyes, their skin a scaly green. For a few seconds there was no movement and no sound, except a low gurgling noise...almost a growl emerging from the creatures all around them.

In the next instant, the one in front of Lian made the first move toward him, and the other three followed suit attacking Gabriel. Lian decided his best chance to survive was to fight back, so he charged the creature, grabbed his legs, and tackled him down to the sand. He turned his body as quickly as he could to come face to face with his opponent. The ghastly sight of the reptilian's face was enough to scare Lian, especially its eyes...the snake-like vertical slits he saw before. His inner strength was returning, and he concentrated on trying to grab the creature's wrists to hold him down and keep from being struck. With every bit of strength, he could muster up, he pushed down on its wrists, but the reptilian threw off Lian's arms as if they were nothing. The creature now moved its hands around Lian's throat. The sheer, raw power of his opponent was obvious as its grip tightened. Suddenly, a loud scream emerged from the reptilian as it quickly pulled its hands back. Lian was confused at first, but then quickly realized his medallion was now glowing brightly had somehow burned the creature. Without haste, he grabbed the medallion and pushed it onto the reptilian's forehead. A burning sound followed by a devastating scream echoed around the rocks, and the reptilian moved no more. Lian paused to see if the creature would come to, but it did not move.

Lian's concentration now moved to Gabriel, who had the other three reptilians on top of him. Two of them had Gabriel's hands pinned down, and the third had some sort of weapon drawn and positioned right above Gabriel's chest. As if he had super speed, Lian flew over and immediately kicked the weapon out of the reptilian's hand, sailing it over toward the water. He then jumped on the creature's back to yank it off Gabriel. One sweep of its arm sent Lian flying through the air, his face landing hard in the sand. Climbing off Gabriel, the reptilian now moved in on a dazed Lian, who was lying crumpled a few yards away. Just then, the beach lit up like it was daytime. A zapping sound echoed through the air, and all three reptilians grabbed their ears as if in pain. When Lian and Gabriel looked at the ocean to see the source of the bright light, a huge flash lit up each of the reptilians. The creatures glowed increasingly brighter, and then disintegrated into the night air. Both boys froze and stared at each other in amazement at what they'd just witnessed.

They turned once again to catch the source of the light and the killing ray. Three brilliantly white circles were hovering above the water. Behind each circle was a faint outline of something humanoid in a long white robe. Each of these figures appeared on some sort of floating disk. And as fast as they appeared, they vanished just as quickly into the ocean.

"The Guardians." Lian gasped under his breath. He jumped to his feet, and ran over to shake Gabriel, whose eyes were still transfixed on the scene unfolding before them. "Come on. We've got to get out of here," pulling on Gabriel's shirt to get him to follow.

The two ran back to their four-wheelers knowing they had to get to the only place that made sense to them at this time, the Lost Cave. A voice broke the silence on the beach.

"Boys. Is everything all right down there?"

Chapter Thirty-five

A Glimmer of Proof

Professor Snodgrass was standing on the bluff stretching his head out and overlooking the area of the beach where Lian and Gabriel had just approached with their four-wheelers.

"I said, are you okay down there, boys?" The professor's voice was noticeably louder this time.

Lian cupped his hands around his mouth, "Yes, Professor. But, we could use your help."

"I'll be right down there. Hold on."

The professor disappeared from sight, and Lian and Gabriel started walking toward the area where they fought the reptilians.

Gabriel looked at Lian, who looked remarkably calm.

"You think we should tell him everything, Lian?"

"I don't know anyone else we could trust with any of the details of what we've just been through. Do you?"

"No. No one." Gabriel shrugged his shoulders and slowly shook his head back and forth.

"Nobody's going to believe the story about the three evaporating. It's too unbelievable. Amazingly enough I'm really not too concerned about that."

"What do you mean? I am not sure if anyone in the world has ever seen, much less reported such a thing. This is *big* news. The whole world should know what we witnessed here tonight. Why wouldn't you be concerned?"

"I said I am not *too* concerned. I'm still thinking about that too, but more concerned about the one killed right over there." Lian pointed at the spot where the reptilian met its fate.

As Lian and Gabriel cautiously approached the dead reptilian in the dark, they noticed something strange about its appearance.

"It's a man. It must have shape-shifted...changed back to its other form."

"How did it happen so quickly?" Gabriel scratched his brow.

"I don't know, but do you understand what this means? We are going to look like murderers."

"Where are you, boys?" yelled the professor.

"We're over by the beach." Gabriel yelled, quickly turning to Lian, "Are you sure we should say something about this, even to Snodgrass?"

"Who else could we trust? Besides...it's a little late now, don't you think?"

"Yeah...we have no choice now."

Excited and scared, Lian and Gabriel started running toward Snodgrass. "You've got to see this, Professor."

As soon as they reached him, the boys felt a great deal of relief escape them.

"Thank you so much for coming. You've got to help us." Lian pleaded, as they each grabbed an arm, and quickly led the professor towards the beach. "So much has happened tonight."

"Okay, boys, okay. I'd like to hear about it."

"Come on, Professor. Hurry. Lian and I need to show you something."

They quickly took turns trying to tell the professor about their exploits. The professor stumbled onto his knees in the sand, but the boys picked him up and continued on. As they approached the spot on the beach where the body was located, Lian pulled back suddenly and stopped everybody.

"Hey. Where did it go?" Lian gasped. "This is the spot, isn't it?"

"Yeah, this is it."

The body was gone without a trace of it ever being there. Gabriel was moving his head quickly from side to side in disbelief, and Lian was running in small bursts in all directions searching the sand's surface.

"I can't believe it." Gabriel threw his hands to the side of his head.

"What are you looking for?" asked the professor. "Are you sure this is the right place?"

"Yeah, it was right here. I mean *right here.*" Lian pointed down at the sand with both index fingers.

"Once again...what are you two looking for? What was here?"

Gabriel held his open palms out, "Professor Snodgrass...there was a body...right here, and it..."

"Hold it," interrupted Lian, walking toward the water to investigate a reflection of an object. When he recognized it as the reptilian's weapon, he hurried over and picked it up carefully. "This is the proof we needed."

"Of course...the weapon. I forgot about that."

"Another couple hours and this thing would have been lost in the tide." Lian handed the object to Snodgrass.

"Boys. You're going to have to slow down. You've said something about a missing body, and now we have a weapon of sorts coming into play. What kind of weapon is this?" Snodgrass looked it over, studying each part.

The two friends looked at each other. Gabriel nodded at Lian to take the lead in bringing the professor up to speed with the night's events.

"Well, Professor...most of this would be unbelievable, and if it wasn't for that weapon, we would have absolutely no proof any of this really happened."

Professor Snodgrass grabbed Lian's upper right arm. "What do you say we just start from the top?"

Chapter Thirty-six

The Fallen One

Professor Snodgrass had his glasses off, cleaning them with his shirt, as he listened intensely to Lian retelling the accounts of the evening. When Lian had finished, the professor sat quietly as he looked back and forth at Lian and then Gabriel. He slipped his glasses back on, and stood up, brushing the sand off his wrinkled pants. Both boys followed suit.

"And you are asking me what you should do."

Lian and Gabriel moved their heads in agreement.

"Well, I will say this...the less said about tonight, the better for everybody. Is it safe to say none of us completely understand what has transpired here tonight? Trying to explain what we don't understand will only complicate things. Do you follow me?"

"I'm sure we both agree with that." Gabriel looked at Lian.

"I would like to take this weapon with me and see if I can do some research on it, maybe perform a few tests. Maybe doing so will help us make sense out of what happened here tonight. Would that be okay with you?"

"Yes sir. I don't want anything to do with it, Professor."

"Me neither." added Gabriel.

"Alright. As for the rest of the story, we tell no one. We need to figure this out, but we need to do it ourselves...without outside help. Understood?"

"Yes, sir."

"Okay, I'll head home with this gadget. Are you two going to be alright here when I leave?"

"We'll be fine, Professor. We've got our four-wheelers over there, and we're heading out of here soon." Lian pointed toward their vehicles.

Snodgrass started walking away, and turned back around abruptly. "Remember boys, there are some things best left alone."

Lian and Gabriel watched the professor leave the beach as they slowly headed to their four-wheelers. Right as they started to mount them, the sky opened up and rain came down in buckets. The boys knew only one place that could give them shelter from the sudden storm, and they ran as fast as they could in the wet sand. They did not stop till they reached the inside of the cave. Lian immediately slid down the side of the cave wall, closed his eyes, and tried to catch his breath. This night seemed like a strange dream he hoped would be over when he opened his eyes, but it didn't disappear. The storm seemed to pick up intensity, and he could hear the waves crashing outside and the rain slapping the sand. He looked toward the cave opening always beckoning him as a place of safety, a place surrounding him like a cocoon. Lian worried the cave would never be a safe haven again if the reptilians ever discovered it. He heard a small shuffle and the flick of a lighter, as Gabriel lit one the small lanterns they had kept hidden behind some rocks.

Lian looked up as the light danced on the walls of the cave. He then remembered how the hieroglyphic figures on the wall almost seemed to dance with the flickering light when he was younger. Now he could make out only a couple scattered lines on the wall. Lian got up to examine the cave wall closely, lightly touched it, and more lines appeared. He started rubbing back and forth on the surface, wider and wider strokes, applying more pressure with each swipe. With a deep breath he blew the gray dust from the area he just rubbed. Waving his hand in front of his face to keep the cloud of dust from reaching him, he stepped back to see what had been revealed. Lian looked at the crude drawings resembling childlike stick figures, the same ones he had seen many times on the wall, when he and Gabriel had first discovered their "Lost Cave." His eyes ran across the various drawings, and he noticed one of them seemed to be floating above the others. It depicted a stick man with a circle drawn around it. He looked over at Gabriel who seemed to be deep in thought as well.

Lian then noticed some more lines below the hieroglyphics he had just opened up. These were not symbols, but words. He started reading them aloud, "A reptilian son who falls and is reborn shall..."

"...destroy all those who were evil before him," Gabriel joined in and was reciting the words from across the cave. Lian stopped reading, shifting his eyes between Gabriel and the words on the wall. Gabriel stared directly into Lian's eyes and continued, "The fallen one will rise."

Silence was the only thing happening in the cave as the rain pelted down on the beach. Lian's tone became more intense. "This writing reminds me of something my mother said to me a long time ago. 'And the Guardians rose from the depths to battle the Trinity.'"

Gabriel moved across the cave, leaned in close to the wall, and looked at the drawing of the stick figure inside a circle.

"There's more." Lian looked down, holding out his necklace. "When she gave me this medallion, she said those exact words. I've never forgotten them, but I've never been able to put them together with anything in my life. That is, before seeing the same words written right here on this wall."

Gabriel's eyes glanced down at the necklace and then back up to Lian's eyes as he followed along.

"This is what saved me tonight," Lian held the medallion higher, "it seemed to burn the one who attacked me."

"Burned him...like he was on fire?"

"Well, it definitely hurt him. He was acting like it was burning all the way through his chest...like from the inside out."

"So you think your medallion has some kind of power?" Gabriel studied Lian's face for his reaction.

"I know it has a protective power, just like my mom said. I just thought she meant protecting me by keeping me from getting hurt, you know? I mean, in everyday life, like on the playground when I was little, or crossing the street, or while I was playing soccer...those kinds of things. Now, I don't know exactly what *else* it can do, and what powers it holds."

Gabriel turned and sat down facing Lian straight on. "I think the time has come to tell you something. I should have told you this before, but I never saw the right opportunity to do so until now."

"What are you talking about?" Lian suddenly felt torn between wanting to know and being afraid to hear. How could anything top what had happened tonight? He looked at the candlelight dancing in his friend's eyes. "What is it?"

"What it is, my friend, is an old saying...an oracle if you will, passed down through my family for a very long time. I've never really believed any of it to be true. But after tonight..."

"After tonight, what?"

Gabriel paused, shifting his body to lean against a rock. "I've learned a few facts from my mother as well. She revealed to me there were some ancient writings from a race of people known as the Pleiadians, better known to you now as the Guardians." Gabriel shifted the attention towards the wall and the circle drawing again. "It looks familiar, doesn't it? I now know exactly who we saw tonight."

"The Guardians? Those were the Guardians?"

"I'm sorry, but I couldn't let on to you about any of this until now." Gabriel now looked down and closed his eyes as he continued. "'A reptilian son who falls and is reborn shall destroy all those who were evil before him.'" Gabriel lifted his eyes to meet Lian's stare. "Does this all make sense to you now?"

Lian became silent, hanging on every word, hearing his mind whirring with scores of questions and possible answers. He leaned his head on the wall, staring at the figures. *Was all of this supposed to make sense?*

"The change you went through at the soccer match." Gabriel looked for a reaction. "How about all those things we found concerning your family...why so many secrets?"

Lian's thoughts now embraced his great-grandfather...his *real* great-grandfather. His name, O. Rion Hunter, his murder, all it so mysterious, as was his father's silence about his heritage. There *were* a lot of family secrets. *Reptilian son? Was he one of them?* He looked down at his hands-so thick, just like his father. His mind now shifted to his mother and her side of the family. They were so different from his father's lineage. He had heard a few stories, but why did she rarely speak about her relatives, her background? Why did Gabriel's mom have the same mannerisms, the same angelic look about her? His mother's face flashed through his mind.

"Still not convinced? Then think about this…you discovered *and* destroyed the reptilian labyrinth." Gabriel put both of his hands on Lian's shoulders. "*You chose* not to join them."

Lian looked up at Gabriel, his eyes widened.

"Lian...you *are* the Fallen One."

Chapter Thirty-seven

The Ascent

Ascent - uh-sent Noun
1. an act of ascending; upward movement; a rising movement:
2. movement upward from a lower to a higher state, degree, grade, or status; advancement:
3. the act of climbing or traveling up:
4. the way or means of ascending; upward slope; acclivity.
5. a movement or return toward a source or beginning.

"You are not wrong who deem
that my days have been a dream;
Yet if hope has flown away
in a night, or in a day,
in a vision, or in none,
is it therefore the less gone?
All that we see or seem
is but a dream within a dream."
— Edgar Allan Poe

Lian opened his eyes, 6:29A.M. He sat up and walked over to the window. The ocean was lapping at the edge of the beach as the sun's bright light gleamed on the water. Lian stretched his arms above his head. He walked into his bathroom and turned on the faucet, letting the cold water run over his hands. As he splashed water on his face, his mom's voice echoed through the door.

"Lian, are you awake?"

He raised his head and looked at the reflection staring back at him in the mirror. He paused for a moment. "Yes…I am," he said to himself.

Lian grabbed a towel and walked back into his bedroom. He looked over at the green jacket hanging on the chair. The scent of crepes drifted in from downstairs, and he breathed in deeply.

"Lingonberry."

C.L. Hagely is an American author.

Made in the USA
San Bernardino, CA
18 December 2016